NOTE

"Get gold. Humanely if possible, but at all costs get gold."

—King Ferdinand II of the Spanish
Kingdom of Aragón (1452–1516)

This story is a work of fiction. However, it is based on historical fact. In the centuries following the Mexican conquest by Hernán Cortés in the early 1500s, an immense and unmeasurable river of gold and silver flowed from Mexico to Spain aboard fleets of Spanish galleons.

So rich were the sources of these precious metals, and so great was the Spanish appetite for them, that it was common for galleons to be overloaded with treasure and other goods, making them difficult to sail in the best of conditions, and particularly vulnerable in bad seas.

As a result, Spanish ships sank with such frequency that a fleet of salvagers was commissioned to recover treasure and goods from any sunken galleon that was deemed reachable. Native divers from Mexico and Central America were routinely used by these salvagers, and it was during this era that the use of a diving bell was first recorded in the western hemisphere.

The Diving Bell

The Diving Bell

Todd Strasser

AN AUTHORS GUILD BACKINPRINT.COM EDITION

The Diving Bell

AN AUTHORS GUILD BACKINPRINT.COM EDITION

Published by iUniverse, Inc.

For information address:
iUniverse, Inc.
2021 Pine Lake Road, Suite 100
Lincoln, NE 68512
www.iuniverse.com

ISBN: 0-595-34491-7

Printed in the United States of America

ONE

Culca squatted in the small dugout canoe, holding a thin rope in her hands. Although it was still early morning, the sun was already hot on her thick black hair, and a slight breeze cooled her almond-colored skin. The lagoon's surface was smooth and the water so clear that Culca could look down through it and see her brother Tulone as he swam below.

The rope jerked and Culca began to pull it up, eager to see what Tulone had put in the shell basket. A moment later Tulone surfaced and pulled himself into the canoe. His wet black hair clung to his head and his chest heaved as he caught his breath.

"What did you find?" Culca asked.

"Two old gray oysters," her brother said. "Probably too old to have pearls."

He was teasing her. The older an oyster was, the larger the pearl it might contain. The basket came to the surface and

1

Tulone plucked out a dripping oyster shell and quickly cut it open. Inside was a pinkish white pearl. It shimmered in the sunlight.

"It's perfect!" Culca gasped.

Tulone smiled broadly. He opened the second oyster and found another pearl, almost identical to the first.

"You must be very lucky," Tulone said. He pressed the pearls into Culca's hand.

"But they're yours," Culca protested. "You found them."

"Keep them," her brother said, "until Mother lets you dive for pearls of your own."

They heard a shout. A boy named Haab had waded partway into the shallow lagoon and waved to them. "Tulone, the divers are leaving! Culca, your mother says it is time to work!"

"I'll never find pearls like these," Culca said with a shake of her head. "Mama will never let me dive."

They returned to their village. Tulone joined the other divers as they pushed their outriggers through the surf, and paddled toward the deep reef where the nacre shells were found. Culca stood on the shore and watched. Near her, three old fishermen sat in a circle, using cotton string and needles made from fish bones to mend a fishing net. Their skin was dark and leathery from many years in the sun.

"Culca!" her mother shouted behind her."Come to work."

Culca's mother, Coatlicue, was standing beside a cotton tarp stretched between three palm trees. In the shade under the tarp, women and girls wearing white smocks mashed corn into paste.

Culca walked slowly up the beach and joined them. She sat down before a flat grinding stone and began to crush the yellow kernels of corn. Around her the women cooked the corn paste into flat round tortillas. They chattered about their aches and pains, the course of the stars, and the mealiness of that year's sweet potato crop. The other girls Culca's age listened carefully, as if trying to learn what being grown-up was like. But Culca paid no attention. Instead she slid her hand into the pocket of her smock and touched the pearls Tulone had given her. She turned to look at the outriggers, now small brown specks on the broad blue sea. How she wished she were a diver, gliding like a fish around the purple and green corals of the deep reef....

"Stop dreaming, Culca," Coatlicue snapped.

The other women paused in their conversations and stared at her. The village girls gig-gled.

"She wants to be a diver like her brother," Culca's mother told the others. "Since when do women dive? What will her husband do? Make tortillas?"

The women chuckled. Even Culca smiled. It was funny to picture a man bent over a grinding stone crushing corn.

"I can't wait to have a husband," said a pretty girl named Ixchel, who had recently completed the ceremony of puberty. "Every day I beg my father to choose the one I will marry."

"Then you will rise early each morning to make your husband's breakfast, mash corn and weave all day, and cook his dinner," said a bitter woman named Tikal. "And after dinner you will scrape salt to sell at the market."

"That's what we're supposed to do," Ixchel said. "It's what we're good at."

Culca watched the women around her nod. "But I'm good at diving," she said. "If we're supposed to do what we're good at, why can't I dive?"

No one answered Culca's question.

The sun rose higher. Soon it was too hot to sit near the hearth where the tortillas were cooking. The women began to get up and go into the weaving house, where they would work until late afternoon when dinner preparations would begin. Culca got up and glanced toward the outriggers.

"Look!" she said, pointing toward the sea.

The fishermen stopped mending their nets and stared out across the turquoise water. The outriggers had raised their sails and were headed for shore.

"It's too early to come in," said an old woman named Faina. "Something is wrong."

"The sharks maybe," said one of the fishermen. Culca saw the wrinkles on Coatlicue's forehead deepen with fear. Just the year before, Culca's cousin had been killed by a shark while diving over the deep reef.

Then Culca saw a tiny speck of white on the horizon behind the outriggers.

"A ship!" she yelled.

"The Spanish!" one of the fishermen said. "That's why the divers are coming in."

Coatlicue grabbed Culca's hand and pulled.

"Come, Culca!" she shouted. Around them the other islanders had started to hurry. Culca followed her mother into their hut.

"Gather the blankets," Coatlicue said quickly. "I'll get the smocks."

"Why?" Culca asked.

"I'll explain later," Coatlicue said. "Now, hurry!"

Moments later, their arms full of blankets and clothes, Culca and her mother ran to the edge of the jungle behind the beach. All around them islanders were hiding their possessions in the thick green underbrush.

"Why is everyone so frightened?" Culca asked.

"No questions now," her mother said as she hid their blankets behind a fallen log.

When the islanders had hidden everything of value, they ran back to the beach. The outriggers drew nearer and the white sails of the Spanish ship grew larger behind them. Soon the outriggers were only a few hundred yards from shore and Culca could see Tulone and the other divers straining as they paddled.

Moments later the outrigger carrying Culca's brother splashed through the surf. Tulone hopped out, his long black hair stiff and stringy from the seawater.

"Run!" Coatlicue told him.

Tulone and the other divers ran into the jungle. Meanwhile the village women gathered the brown and black nacre shells that were lined with mother-of-pearl. They buried them quickly in the sand while the fishermen threw nets and fish into the outriggers to make them look like fishing boats.

By now the Spanish ship was so close that Culca could see the bright red crosses on the billowing white sails, and the long gold and blue banners flapping from the yardarms. The ship's hull was painted with green and white checks, and many cannons protruded from the gun ports. As Culca stood on the beach, she could feel the fear in those around her. Why? she wondered. Why is everyone so afraid?

Two

Culca's people were small, but strong. They had broad shoulders and thick arms and legs. Living on a diet of fish, corn, sweet potatoes, and fruit, they were rarely sick.

They had lived on their island off the Yucatán peninsula on the eastern coast of Mexico for nearly a thousand years. At one time Culca's ancestors had been part of the great Mayan civilization that stretched across much of Mexico and Central America. But war had splintered the empire and what remained was weakened further by the Spanish who came to spread Christianity and search for gold and other treasures.

The Spaniards who came to Culca's island had forced the islanders to build a small church on the hill behind the village. The church was made of stones and had a wooden cross on its roof. A thin, white-haired friar who walked barefoot and wore coarse brown robes had stayed behind. He was ordered to teach the villagers the Spanish ways. The Spanish sailors had

warned Culca's people that if anything happened to the friar, they would pay dearly for it. When the villagers saw that the friar had no weapons and did not appear dangerous, they left him alone.

As Culca and the others watched the Spanish ship approach, the friar made one of his rare journeys to the beach.

"Why are they coming?" Culca asked him.

The friar pressed his thin lips together and shook his head. "I don't know," he replied in the language of the village.

"We have coconuts to give them," said the village chief, holding a green coconut in each hand. He was a fat, silly man who had once been a very good diver, but the diver's sickness had made his mind feeble. Still, the villagers let him remain chief. Now that the Spanish ruled, there was little for a chief to do.

"I'm afraid they're not coming for coconuts," the friar said with a sigh. To Culca, he seemed like a sad and lonely man. He had been left on the island to teach the Spanish ways, but the villagers weren't interested. Instead, the friar had to learn the islanders' language and ways.

Two hundred yards from shore the Spanish ship let down an anchor and prepared a longboat to sail to the beach. The friar turned to Culca's mother.

"Take your daughter away," he said. "She is a pretty girl and one never knows what my countrymen will do."

"Come, Culca," Coatlicue said. "We will go to the hut."

But Culca didn't move. "I want to see," she said. "The last time the Spanish came I was so young I don't remember."

"You'll watch from the hut," her mother said sternly.

Culca walked slowly up the beach. Behind her the long-boat came toward the shore, rowed by men of different colors. Some were nearly as dark as the nacre shells. Others were the almond color of Culca's people. Still others had skin that was almost as light as the Spaniards themselves. But all wore chains and shackles around their wrists. Culca stood in the entrance to her hut and watched.

"Why are they wearing chains?" she asked her mother.

"Because they're slaves," said Coatlicue.

"What's a slave?" Culca asked.

"Someone who is kept like a goat and worked like an ox."

Culca have never seen an ox or a goat, but she had heard stories of those animals from the men who went to the mainland market to trade goods from the village.

"That's terrible," Culca said. "Why do the slaves allow it?"

"The Spanish will kill them if they disobey," Coatlicue explained.

Culca was shocked. "They wouldn't!"

Coatlicue nodded sadly. "Nothing has been right since the Spanish arrived."

By the time the longboat touched the shore, the beach was deserted except for the friar and the village chief. The rest of the villagers stood in front of their huts, and watched warily.

A tall Spanish officer with reddish hair stepped off the boat.

"Look at the color of his hair!" Culca whispered to her mother. "And how tall he is."

"Evil comes in many different forms," Coatlicue whispered back.

Four soldiers wearing helmets and carrying muskets followed the officer onto the beach. The village chief offered them the coconuts, but the officer slapped the nuts to the ground and sent the chief scurrying away. Then he spoke to the friar in a loud angry voice. Culca could not understand what was said, but the friar shook his head several times.

The officer turned and shouted orders at the soldiers, who ran to the village outriggers and began flinging out nets and fish carcasses. One of the soldiers found something and ran back toward the officer. To Culca it looked like an oyster shell. The officer inspected the shell, then wheeled around, striking the friar in the face with the back of his hand. Culca gasped as the friar tumbled to the sand.

"Why did the officer strike him?" she asked.

"I don't know," Coatlicue whispered.

The officer shouted more orders and the soldiers started toward the village.

"Come, Culca!" Coatlicue grabbed Culca's hand and pulled her out of their hut.

All the islanders began to run toward the jungle. Culca and Coatlicue made their way through the long green vines and thick underbrush and found a palm tree to hide behind. Looking back, they watched in horror as the roof of a hut burst into flames. Then the hut next to it began to burn.

"They're burning our homes!" Culca cried.

"Shhhh." Coatlicue held her finger to her lips.

"Why can't we stop them?" Culca asked. "There are only five of them and many more of us."

"If we fight them, more will come with horses and cannons," said an old fisherman named Batab, who was stooped behind a tree near them. "For each Spaniard we kill, they will kill ten of us."

Another hut began to burn. Culca looked at the villagers crouching among the vines and brush, their faces filled with fright and helpless anger as they watched their homes burn.

"Then we are slaves, too." she said.

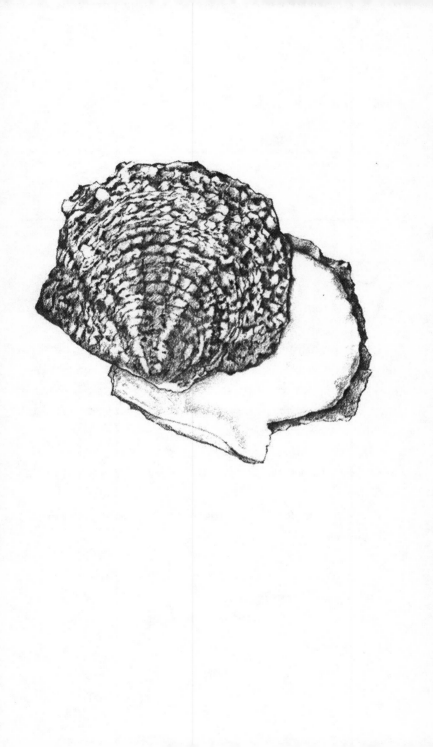

THREE

When all the huts had been set on fire, the Spanish soldiers boarded the longboat and sailed back to their ship.

That night the islanders slept on the beach. Behind them the roofs of their huts still smoldered. As Culca lay curled up and shivering on the sand, she looked at the stars twinkling in the black sky. It was not easy to fall asleep, and when she did, she did not sleep for long.

In the middle of the night she woke with a start. Something heavy was scratching her leg as it crawled up her calf.

"Mama!" Culca cried in the dark, twisting and kicking the thing away.

Coatlicue and Tulone woke up. "What is it, Culca?"

"I don't know." Culca's heart was racing. The thing kept scratching and scraping.

Tulone crawled toward it in the dark.

"What is it, Tulone?"

"Something bad," Tulone said. "Very bad."

"What? What?" Coatlicue gasped.

"A terrible thing."

"What? Tell us!"

"Look!" Laughing, Tulone held up a land crab.

"Oh, Tulone, you teased us," Coatlicue said angrily.

"It's all right," Tulone said gently. "You can go to sleep." He tossed the crab far away.

"Sleep next to me," Culca said.

Tulone lay down near her. "That crab was probably more frightened than you, little sister," he whispered. In the moonlight Culca could see his broad, bright smile.

"Go to sleep, you two," Coatlicue said. "We have a lot to do in the morning."

Culca closed her eyes and tried to sleep, but her heart was still beating from the fright. She opened her eyes and found Tulone staring at her.

"Don't worry," he whispered. "The crab won't come back."

"It's not the crab I'm thinking about," Culca whispered. "It's the Spanish."

Tulone nodded slowly. "There's nothing we can do about them. Try to sleep."

Culca shut her eyes, but sleep did not come easily that night.

*   *   *

The next day the islanders began to repair their huts. The men climbed high into the palms and chopped down the pointed green fronds to use for new thatching. The women threaded the intricate webbing for new hammocks by hand. Culca and her mother and brother were sweeping the charred remains out of their hut when Faina came with the old fisherman Batab and the young boy Haab.

"We need food for dinner," Faina said.

"Batab and I will catch fish," Tulone said.

"I'm going, too," said Haab. He was only eight, but when the sea was calm he went with the fishermen.

"Can I go?" Culca asked her mother.

"You must help with the hammocks."

"But I want to go fishing," Culca begged. "Please?"

"No." Coatlicue shook her head.

"If Tulone and Haab can go, why can't I?" Culca asked.

"Because I said so," Coatlicue replied firmly.

"It's not fair." Culca turned and ran down the beach to the water's edge. There she sat on the sand with her fists clenched in anger. She saw a shadow and looked up. Ixchel and another girl stood behind her.

16

"You must do as you're told, Culca," Ixchel said in a teasing voice.

"Who says?" Culca asked.

"Everyone."

"That's no reason," Culca replied.

The girls giggled. Culca felt her cheeks burn.

"Go away, you two," someone shouted. Culca saw Tulone coming toward them. Ixchel and her friend ran away laughing. Tulone squatted beside Culca on the sand.

"I'm sorry you can't come fishing," he said.

Culca nodded. "It's not your fault."

"If it were up to me, you would fish and dive every day," her brother said.

Culca smiled at him. Then she saw Coatlicue and Faina coming. Faina was wrinkled and old. Her hair was turning white—the symbol of wisdom.

"Why don't you listen to your mother?" Faina asked Culca.

"Tulone is going fishing because he doesn't want to thatch," Culca said. "If I don't want to weave, I should be able to go, too."

"She's just like her father," Coatlicue said with a sigh. "He only wanted to dive and fish."

"Girls are supposed to cook and weave," Faina said.

"Why?" Culca asked.

17

"It's the will of the gods," said Faina. "You must obey."

"The gods send the Spanish to take our things," Culca replied. "Yet we disobey and hide them."

Faina looked at Culca, and then out at the turquoise sea. She thought a moment and then turned back to Coatlicue.

"I understand why you are afraid to let your daughter go," Faina said. "But she'll be more useful as an eager fisherman than as a reluctant weaver."

Coatlicue frowned. Culca could see her mother wasn't happy with the decision, but Faina was the wisest person in the village.

"I'll make sure she is safe," Tulone said, putting his arm around his sister's shoulder.

"All right," Coatlicue said to her daughter. "You can go fishing just this once."

All morning Culca, Tulone, Haab, and Batab fished with nets. By noon the bottom of their outrigger was covered with fish.

"That's enough," Batab said as he reached for the outrigger's sail. "If we catch any more, I'm afraid we'll sink."

Culca hated to stop fishing. She loved being out in the boat with the sunlight sparkling on the water and the cool breeze on her skin. But as Batab raised the sail her thoughts turned to the Spanish and the questions no one had answered the day before.

"When did the Spanish first come?" she asked Batab as the sail filled with wind and began to take them home.

"When I was a boy," the old fisherman said, "the Spanish came in their great wooden ship. We had never seen such men—some with hair so fair and eyes so round and blue we thought they must be gods. To please them we offered jade, and green and red quetzal feathers. But we soon learned they only wanted gold."

"Why gold?" Haab asked. "It's too soft to use for tools and fishhooks."

"The Spanish love gold," said Batab. "They will do anything to get it. To find out if we had any gold, they burned my father's feet with hot coals and held the village chief underwater until he nearly drowned. But we have no gold on this island and they soon left."

"But they came back," Tulone said.

"Yes," said the old fisherman. "The next time the Spanish ship came, we boarded our outriggers and tried to drive it away. We shot many arrows, but then the ship fired a cannon. It made a noise like thunder and an outrigger burst apart. One of our warriors was torn to pieces and two others were thrown into the sea.

"The Spanish came to shore on horses. They fired muskets and killed our people from a great distance. We knew many would be killed, so we didn't resist. The Spanish took whatever they wanted."

"But yesterday we hid the things they wanted," Culca said.

"There are certain things our village must keep in order to survive," Batab said.

"But then the Spanish burn our huts," Tulone said.

Batab nodded. Culca was confused.

"Next time we should give them some blankets," she said. "It would be easier to replace a few blankets than rebuild our huts."

"Blankets are not what the Spanish want," Batab said. Then he turned and said no more.

The sun was high overhead when they returned to the village.

"Who wants to go diving in the lagoon?" Tulone asked as they pulled the outrigger up on the beach.

"I do," said Culca.

"Wait, Culca," said Batab. "Someone must help me clean the fish before they spoil."

Culca was disappointed, but she knew Batab was right. Besides, if she did a good job, perhaps her mother would let her fish again.

"What about you, Haab?" Tulone asked. "Want to go diving?"

"I don't know how to dive," the boy said.

"Then I'll teach you," said Tulone.

Haab shook his head. "My mother says it's too dangerous. She doesn't want me to get the diving sickness."

"Not all divers get the sickness," Tulone said.

"Some get eaten by sharks," said Haab.

"All right," said Tulone. "If no one wants to go, then I'll go alone."

Tulone left and Haab went off to play. Culca helped Batab clean the fish and soak the fillets in lime juice. When each fillet was finished, they laid it on a board to cook in the hot sun. Coatlicue came to look at the catch.

"Your daughter handles a fishing net well," Batab said.

"Can I fish again tomorrow?" Culca asked.

"No," Coatlicue answered.

"But Faina said—"

"Faina doesn't understand," Coatlicue said.

"She's the wisest person in the village," said Culca.

Coatlicue squatted down beside her daughter. "You are young and there are many things I haven't told you. But perhaps the time has come."

"What kind of things?" Culca asked.

"You never knew your father," Coatlicue said sadly. "I told you he died of sickness, but the truth is the Spanish took him."

"Why?" Culca asked.

"The Spanish fill their ships with treasure and other goods," said Batab. "Then they sail the ships back to their homeland across the sea. But sometimes a storm comes and a ship sinks. Then all the treasure goes to the bottom. The Spanish use our divers to bring up their treasure."

"Why didn't my father return once the treasure was found?" Culca asked.

"Sometimes there are sharks," said Batab. "And it's said that the Spanish work the divers very hard and treat them poorly."

"Why?" Culca asked.

"That I cannot tell you," Batab said, shaking his head.

"I can't stop Tulone from diving," Coatlicue said. "He's a young man and the best diver in our village. We need him."

"Without mother-of-pearl to trade at market, we would have no rope for our boats and no knives to clean fish," Batab added.

"But you're a girl and can be helpful in many other ways," Coatlicue said. "That is why I don't want you to dive."

Culca's mother stood up and returned to her work. Culca turned to Batab.

"Hasn't there ever been a girl who wanted to dive?" she asked.

Batab shook his head. "Not that I can remember, Culca."

FOUR

That night Culca lay down to sleep on the floor of her hut with her mother and brother. The thatching work had gone slowly that day and none of the roofs had yet been repaired, nor were the hammocks finished. The night air was heavy with moisture and the dark sky was filled with thick clouds. As Culca gazed at the clouds she wondered about her father and wished she could remember him. But she was only a baby when the Spanish took him away. It made her sad to think that he had died for the sake of Spanish treasure.

The sky flashed with lightning and rumbled with thunder. Rain began to splash down on Culca's face. She cowered under her blanket, but soon the floor became muddy and it was impossible to sleep. Coatlicue and Tulone sat up.

"What shall we do?" Culca's mother asked.

Tulone shivered. "We could go into the jungle."

"It's too dangerous at night," Coatlicue said.

"What about the church?" Culca asked.

Tulone and Coatlicue glanced at each other. "We've never been inside the church," Tulone said.

"I have many times," Culca said. "The friar won't hurt you."

The rain fell harder. Culca could see that Coatlicue and Tulone were nervous about going to the church, but they were also cold and wet.

"All right," Tulone said, getting up. "We'll go."

As they walked along the muddy path up the hill, Culca thought about her other visits to the church. The islanders were kind people, and since the friar was thin and frail they often gave him food. Culca always offered to carry the food to the church as an excuse not to crush corn or weave. Sometimes she found the friar sitting inside, reading by candlelight. Sometimes, when the sun was shining, she found him outside, tending his small garden of beans and squash.

Once when Culca visited the friar she found him standing on a table inside the church. At first she assumed this was some odd Spanish custom, but then she noticed that the friar was trembling and looked very frightened.

"Watch out!" he shouted at her. "There's a dragon!"

"Where?" Culca asked.

"It was there." The friar pointed a shaking finger at the wooden pew nearest the altar. "A huge one. Oh, merciful Lord, please make it leave!"

Culca went to look.

"Where are you going?" the friar cried. "Don't go near it!" But Culca was curious. She stepped slowly toward the altar, trying to imagine just what a dragon would look like and how large it could possibly be. Suddenly she stopped. On the floor under the pew was a long green-scaled tail with reddish spines sticking out. Culca bent down for a closer look. The "dragon" stuck its black forked tongue out at her. It had large black eyes, green wrinkled skin, and horns growing from its head. It was only an iguana. Culca quickly grabbed its tail and pulled it toward the door. The iguana clawed the dirt floor of the church and tried to shake loose from her grip.

"What are you doing?" the friar cried. "Don't touch it! You'll be bitten! Careful!"

Culca dragged the struggling lizard out of the church and down the path of the village. Several times she had to stop and yank its claws free from tree trunks and roots. Finally she pulled it into the weaving house where Coatlicue sat with the other women.

"Culca, where did you find that?" her mother asked with surprise.

"In the church," Culca said. "The friar thought it was a dragon."

The women laughed.

"Well," said Coatlicue, taking the iguana from Culca. "This dragon will make a tasty dinner tonight."

Now Coatlicue and Tulone followed Culca through the storm to the church. Rain splattered against the church roof and dripped from its eaves. Through a small window Culca could see the friar sitting in the light of a candle, reading.

"What if he doesn't want to be disturbed?" Coatlicue asked nervously.

"I don't think he'll mind," Culca replied and rapped on the rough wooden door.

The door opened and the friar looked down at her.

"Ah, Culca the dragon eater," he said with a smile. "How can I help you?"

"The roofs of our huts aren't finished and my people are wet," Culca said.

"Have them come here," said the friar.

Tulone and Coatlicue went back down the hill to get the others. Culca held the church door for them while the friar lit more candles inside. The villagers entered the church slowly. Many had never sat on a bench before or seen a candle. Since they were wet and cold from the rain, the friar made them a warm drink from coconut milk, cocoa beans, and honey. The villagers huddled in the pews, sipping the drink from clay mugs and glancing around curiously. They stared at the image of the Madonna and child, and at the wooden cross with the carved figure of Jesus nailed to it.

"Is there anything more I can do for you?" the friar asked in the native language.

The villagers weren't sure how to answer. After all, he was a Spaniard and they had seen how terrible his people could be.

"Why did the soldiers burn our huts?" Tulone asked.

"They were angry because all the divers ran away into the jungle," the friar explained.

"Why did the tall Spaniard strike you?" Coatlicue asked.

"I told him the village needed its divers to survive," the friar said.

The islanders began to murmur among themselves. Finally Culca said, "You are a good man, Friar. Why are the others so evil?"

"They're not really evil," the friar replied. "They're overcome with greed for the riches your land offers. It makes them forget that we're all God's children."

The islanders had no more questions. Outside the rain began to slow. The villagers waited until the rain stopped, and then started to leave. Culca was surprised when her mother whispered for her to stay behind. She and Coatlicue waited until they and the friar were the only ones left in the church.

"Father, your people took my husband because he was a diver," Culca's mother said. "My son is also a diver and every day I fear I may lose him as well. Now my daughter wants to dive. I tell her no, but she is strong-willed and refuses to do her chores. What can I do?"

In the candlelight, the friar rubbed his chin and thought. Culca prayed he would tell Coatlicue to let her dive. But after a moment he said, "Let her come here every day. I will teach her the ways of God and the knowledge of my countrymen."

Both Culca and Coatlicue were puzzled.

"Why should she learn this?" Coatlicue asked.

"Because the Spanish now rule this land," the friar said. "If your village is to survive, you must understand my people."

Culca didn't know whether she liked this idea or not.

"Can't I dive with Tulone?" she asked.

"I said no," her mother replied sternly.

Culca turned to the friar. "Then I'll learn the Spanish ways."

"Very good." The friar smiled. Culca knew it wasn't what she wanted, but at least it might be more interesting than making tortillas.

FIVE

Each morning the friar gave Culca lessons in religion, mathematics, and the Spanish language. In Culca's religion there were many gods; the most important were the gods of rain, corn, medicine, and the sun. The friar's religion had saints whose roles seemed similar. In Culca's religion all the gods were ruled by a supreme god called *Hunab Ku*. The friar's religion also had a supreme God, but instead of worshiping him with dance and song, the friar taught Culca to pray and chant.

Culca also learned the Spanish language. "*Uno, dos...ocho, nueve, diez,*" she counted from one to ten.

"You learn very quickly," the friar said with a smile. "Perhaps someday you'll teach the others in your village."

Culca nodded, but secretly she still wanted to dive.

Each afternoon after Culca finished her lessons she returned to her hut. Sometimes Coatlicue would ask what she had learned that day.

"I learned to count," Culca said one day.

"But you already know how to count," her mother said.

"In Spanish," Culca explained.

"What's the difference?" Coatlicue shook her head sadly. "You neither cook nor weave. Soon it will be your time for the ceremony of puberty. How will we ever find a husband for you?"

"Let him find me," Culca said.

Her mother rolled her eyes toward the sky. "May the gods be kind to you."

The growing season came. On sunny days the friar gave Culca her lessons in the church and then went outside to tend his garden. Sometimes he spent all day on his hands and knees in the rich brown soil. One day Culca followed him outside.

"Did you have a garden before you came here?" she asked.

"Oh, yes," the friar said. "Ever since I was a small boy I've loved to watch things grow. It's the miracle of life—a tiny seed turning into a plant that bears fruit and food."

Sweat dripped down his forehead and he wiped it with the sleeve of his robe.

"Why do you wear such heavy robes?" Culca asked.

"They are called the livery of labor and I wear them in service to the Lord," the friar replied as he yanked plants out of the ground.

"Why are you killing your plants?" Culca asked.

"These aren't my plants," the friar said as he carefully patted the earth down. "They're weeds and will choke my vegetables if I don't pull them."

"Like the Spanish have choked my people," Culca said.

The friar looked up at her. "Yes, Culca, I'm afraid that's right." Then he returned to his gardening.

Culca had a secret. Whenever the friar left her alone in the church she stopped doing her lessons. Sometimes she played, or daydreamed of diving with Tulone. Sometimes she looked at the books filled with squiggles and dots. Culca knew this was the Spanish way of writing, but it made no sense to her yet.

One day she found a book that fascinated her. The heavy white pages were filled with drawings of things she had never seen before. One was a crossbow like those carried by the Spanish soldiers, but this one was the size of twenty men and carried an arrow the length of a tree trunk. Another showed a chariot with long blades attached to it. When a horse pulled the chariot through a crowd, the blades whirled around chopping people into pieces.

On another page she found drawings of underwater swimmers wearing masks with long pipes leading to the surface.

One drawing showed a man breathing air under a large cone. Culca realized that these devices allowed divers to breathe underwater. She was amazed. Just think of how many nacre shells a diver could gather if he never had to swim to the surface for fresh air!

"What are you doing?" the friar suddenly asked behind her.

Culca jumped. She'd been so absorbed in the book that she hadn't heard him return from the garden. She felt her cheeks burn with shame.

"Curiosity is nothing to be ashamed of," the friar said softly. He tapped the book with a bony finger. "And this is a most curious book. It's the work of an Italian named Da Vinci, a very wise man—although we don't understand many of the things he draws."

Culca had an idea. "Friar, you say it's good to be curious. Aren't you curious about diving?"

The friar thought for a moment. "To be honest, no."

"But you're teaching me what you know," Culca said. "Can't I teach you what I know?"

"But why should I learn to dive?" the friar asked.

"Please!" Culca begged.

The friar frowned. "But your mother…"he began.

"I'm sure she won't mind just this once," Culca said, although she knew this probably wasn't true.

"There's another problem," said the friar. "I don't know how to swim."

Culca was surprised. She'd never heard of someone who couldn't swim. In her village the children learned to swim soon after they learned to walk.

"I grew up in the mountains," the friar explained. "We had a few lakes, but the lake water was very cold. The first time I saw the ocean was the day I boarded the ship to come here."

"What are 'mountains'?" Culca asked.

The friar laughed. "I see there is much for both of us to learn."

Culca kept asking the friar all day and he finally agreed to go out to the deep reef with her. The two of them went down the hill to the ocean. The clear seawater lapped at the sand, darkening it with each wave. Culca chose a dugout canoe because the outriggers were too large for a thin old man and a girl to sail alone. She brought a round diving stone about the size of a coconut, and a shell basket, both tied to long ropes.

The friar climbed uncertainly into the dugout and gripped the sides tightly as Culca pushed the boat through the surf. It was a warm, sunny day and a light breeze made the friar's thin hair flutter over his ears. Once they were past the surf, Culca showed him how to use the short wooden paddles, but the friar paddled awkwardly and without much strength.

By the time Culca and the friar reached the deep reef, the divers were eating lunch. They had tied two outriggers together and placed a board between them to serve as the table. The divers cut open some oysters and squeezed lime juice on the raw food, which they ate along with bananas and pineapple.

"Culca! What are you doing here?" Tulone asked.

"Showing the friar how to dive," Culca explained proudly. She ate a raw oyster and offered one to the friar.

"No, thank you," the friar moaned, nervously holding the sides of the dugout.

"Have you found many shells?" Culca asked her brother.

Tulone pointed to the bottom of his outrigger, where a basket lay half filled with dark nacre shells the size of a large man's hand. The outsides of the shells were rough and covered with barnacles and small growths of coral, but the insides were lined with the smooth, iridescent mother-of-pearl.

"There are many shells in this part of the reef," Tulone said. "We'll fill our baskets before the sun falls."

Seeing the beautiful mother-of-pearl made Culca eager to dive. As soon as lunch was finished, she showed the friar how to lower the shell basket. Then she took deep breaths to build up the air in her lungs and jumped into the water.

"The diving stone, Friar," she said as she held on to the side of the dugout.

The friar lifted the stone and handed it to her. Holding the stone tightly, Culca let go of the dugout and shot quickly downward. She pinched her nose and swallowed to keep the pressure even in her ears. Around her the water grew colder and darker. Pressure pushed her cheeks in and bent her lips back. Soon she reached the reef, with its growths of pink, green, and yellow coral. Some were shaped like huge brains, others like delicate fans, and still others branched out like gnarled tree limbs. Culca began to search for shells. Schools of small purple fish darted in and out of the corals and Culca was careful not to swim too close to the wavy pink lips of a giant clam nearby. Soon she spotted a nacre shell and reached for it, watching carefully for the green moray eels that sometimes shot out of the crevices and clamped their needle sharp teeth around a diver's wrist.

Culca put three shells in the shell basket before she ran out of breath. She tugged on the rope attached to the basket and swam up.

"What did you find?" asked the friar when Culca reached the surface.

"Three good shells," Culca said proudly as she took deep breaths of cool fresh air. Already she was eager to dive again. "Hurry. Empty the shell basket and pull up the diving stone."

"Yes, yes, I'm trying," the friar said as he pulled on the rope attached to the basket. His pale forehead was damp with perspiration and the arms of his robe were dark with seawater. The shell basket broke the surface and the friar dumped the shells on the bottom of the dugout. Then he slowly started to pull up the diving stone.

"Pull faster," Culca said impatiently. Unlike the islanders, who had strong arms and shoulders, the friar's arms were thin and his shoulders narrow. He couldn't pull for long without resting.

"Don't stop," Culca begged.

"I'm sorry, Culca, but I'm not used to this kind of work," the friar said as he rested.

"Then I'll pull up the stone myself," Culca said, grabbing the side of the dugout. In her haste, Culca forgot that the dugout had no outrigger to steady it. As she pulled herself up, the dugout began to tilt. Too late Culca realized what she had done. The dugout flipped over with a loud splash as the friar, the basket, and the nacre shells all disappeared into the water.

The friar doesn't swim, Culca thought. He'll drown! She quickly dived under the water, but the friar was nowhere in sight. She swam to the surface and shouted to the other divers for help. Then she dived again, searching frantically in the water until she was out of breath. But the friar was gone!

The other divers rushed toward her, Tulone was the first to arrive.

"What happened?" he asked as he helped Culca out of the water.

"I tipped it over," Culca cried, pointing to the upside-down dugout. "I can't find the friar."

Tulone quickly dived into the dark blue water. Culca sat in the outrigger and sobbed. She was certain she'd never see the friar again. "It's my fault," she sniffed. "If only I wasn't so impatient."

Suddenly she heard a knocking sound. It seemed to come from the overturned dugout.

Clunk, clunk, clunk! There it was again. Culca stared at the dugout, but it was almost completely submerged. What could be making the sound? She had to find out and dived back into the water.

As she swam toward the upside-down dugout she thought she saw a pair of legs. Could it be? She swam closer. Yes! It was the friar! Culca swam under the dugout. She was amazed to find him clinging to the inside of the dugout and breathing from a pocket of air trapped under the hull.

"I didn't know you had magic, Friar," Culca said, looking around inside the dugout.

"Neither did I." The friar was soaking wet and trembling.

"But you put air here to breathe," Culca said.

"I didn't," said the friar. "It was simply here."

By now Tulone had returned to the surface and swam toward them. He and the other divers helped the friar out of the water and into an outrigger.

The friar was shivering. His wet robes clung to his bony shoulders and his white hair was matted down on his head. Culca squatted near him.

"I'm happy you didn't drown," she said.

"So am I," the friar said, his teeth chattering. "But I'll be even happier when I'm back on dry land."

SIX

"There will be no lesson tomorrow," the friar told Culca one afternoon.

"Why?" Culca asked.

"I'm going to the mainland," he said. "To give a report of my progress to the archdiocese and get new seed for my garden. If all goes well, I'll be back in three days."

"Can I go with you?" Culca asked. Going to the mainland sounded exciting. Besides, if she stayed behind, Coatlicue would make her weave or mash corn.

"I doubt your mother will let you," said the friar.

"She might if you tell her I should go," Culca said. "Tell her I would learn many things."

"Well, that much is true," the friar admitted. "All right, I'll speak to her." Seeing the delight in Culca's eyes made him smile.

Culca and the friar went down to Culca's hut. Inside were two small rooms. In one room three pastel-colored hammocks hung on thick poles. In the other was a small stone hearth and a wooden table. Coatlicue was squatting by the hearth cooking sweet potatoes for dinner. She rose quickly when she saw the friar.

"Mama," Culca said eagerly. "The friar has something to say."

Coatlicue stared quizzically at the friar, who cleared his throat nervously.

"I'm going to the city on the mainland for a few days," he said. "I think it would be good for Culca to come along. She will see the market and the church and the schools the children attend. It's very different from your village."

Coatlicue frowned.

"Oh, Mama, please?" Culca begged.

"What if they make her a slave?" Coatlicue asked the friar.

"They have no reason to make her a slave," the friar replied. "To my people she possesses no special value. She doesn't cook. She's not strong enough to work in the fields. They won't want her."

"She can dive," said Coatlicue.

"They won't know that," the friar said. "And besides, she'll be with me."

"I promise I'll stay close to the friar," Culca assured her mother. "Please, Mama? Please let me go?"

Coatlicue sighed. She didn't understand why her daughter would want to go so far away. But the friar was a good man even if he was a Spaniard, and she trusted him.

"All right, Culca, you may go. But be careful."

"Oh, thank you, Mama!" Culca squealed with delight and kissed her on the cheek.

The next morning right after breakfast Culca ran down to the beach and helped the men load their goods into the largest outrigger. Twice a year they sailed to the mainland to trade mother-of-pearl, salt, dried fish, and stingray spines, which the native medicine men used for bloodletting. In return they got rope, flint, tobacco, cocoa beans, and sharp blades made from obsidian, a kind of glass found near volcanos.

The friar came down the beach, followed by Coatlicue and Tulone. Tulone rubbed Culca's head affectionately.

"Take care, little sister," he said and pressed a small jade carving of a warrior into her hand. "This is for good luck."

Culca smiled and hugged him around the neck. But her mother looked sad.

"Don't worry, Mama, I'll be safe," Culca said.

Coatlicue didn't reply. She only kissed Culca on the forehead.

Culca and the friar boarded the outrigger, and the villagers picked up their paddles and began to row. Culca waved one last time to her mother and brother. The friar kneeled on the bottom of the boat and said a prayer.

Culca and the men paddled all morning. As the island grew smaller and smaller behind them, Culca felt a little queasy. She'd never been out this far in the sea where the water turned dark gray-blue and was many times deeper than a diver could dive. The outrigger cut through the small waves and soon her island was no longer visible. Culca felt a brief pang of regret. Beside her the friar looked pale.

By noon they reached the great channel between the island and the mainland. There they paused to eat bananas and dried fish, and drink fresh water from a gourd. The ocean swells gently lifted and dropped the outrigger, and Culca could see nothing but water and sky in every direction. They had no protection from the hot sun. The friar covered his head with his robe. Despite the bright sun his skin looked almost ashen. He didn't eat lunch and took only a few sips of water.

"Do you feel all right?" Culca asked.

"I'll feel better when there is land beneath my feet," he replied.

All afternoon they paddled across the great channel. The village men told stories of other trips when the sea had been much rougher. Culca was glad the water was smooth because it made paddling easier and she wanted to show the men that she could work as hard as they.

It wasn't until the sun was low and orange that Culca spotted a fringe of green on the horizon. "Look, Friar," she whispered. "Land."

The friar gazed longingly toward the shore. "Ah, heaven," he whispered back.

As they sailed closer they saw a white strip of beach and large stone pyramids protruding from the dark green jungle.

"What are those?" she asked.

"The old worshipping places of the mainland natives," the friar said.

"Do they worship there still?" Culca asked.

"No. The king of Spain has ordered that all natives must now worship in the Spanish church," the friar said.

"Are they forced to?" Culca asked. "Like slaves?"

The friar shook his head. "The king of Spain has proclaimed that your people shall not be forced into slavery."

Culca was confused. "But I saw slaves rowing the Spanish longboat. And the Spaniards took my father against his will."

"The king of Spain is very far away," the friar tried to explain. "He doesn't understand many things about life in the New World. Here the Spanish officially take no slaves...unless they need them."

Dusk was falling by the time they reached the mainland shore. The men pulled the outrigger up on the beach, built a fire in the sand, and ate dinner.

"You're eating more than I am," the friar said as Culca reached for her third potato.

"Today I worked harder than you," Culca replied with a smile.

As the air grew cool and the fire dimmed, they spread their blankets on the beach. Culca wriggled back and forth to make a comfortable spot in the sand. She looked up at the stars sparkling in the night sky and listened to the cries of the animals that lived in the jungle. She felt a little frightened being so far from home. She was also confused. She didn't understand how the Spaniards could make slaves of her people, or why the King of Spain would not allow them to worship their own gods. But she didn't think about it for long. She was tired and quickly fell asleep.

SEVEN

The next morning Culca was awakened by the sun. Near her, the friar woke and rose very stiffly.

"I'm afraid I didn't sleep very well," he groaned, rubbing his neck and back.

"That's because you didn't dig a comfortable place for yourself," Culca said, pointing at the small valleys in the sand she and the men had made.

"There is always more to learn," the friar said with a smile.

After breakfast they pushed the outrigger back into the water and paddled along the shore. In some places the dense jungle grew right to the water's edge. Green and red parrots flew among the branches. Soon a small village appeared ahead. The huts were crude and made of sticks and brush.

As the outrigger approached, a scrawny dog ran down the beach and barked. Then one of the villagers came out of his hut with a bow. He wore a loincloth made from the skin of an animal and his face was painted with red and black stripes. The next thing Culca knew, an arrow whizzed over her head.

"Stay low!" the man behind Culca shouted as he and the others quickly turned the outrigger away from the shore.

Culca ducked down. Another arrow shot past and a third hit the side of the outrigger with a *clunk!* The friar cowered beside Culca in the bottom of the boat as many more arrows flew by. Suddenly one shot past Culca's ear and pierced the friar's robe.

"Friar!" Culca cried. She tried to crawl to him. But one of the villagers grabbed her.

"Stay down or you'll be hit!" he shouted.

"But the friar..." Culca gasped.

"You can't help him now," the man said. More arrows hissed past, splashing into the water around them. The men paddled as hard as they could. Culca crouched lower and hugged her knees. The friar lay on the bottom of the boat and didn't move. Culca felt tears rise in her eyes.

Finally the outrigger sailed out of range and the arrows fell harmlessly into the sea behind them. Culca quickly crawled to the friar.

"Friar?" She tugged at his robe. "Oh, please speak to me."

"Are they gone?" the friar asked, raising his head.

"You're all right?" Culca was amazed.

"Yes, I think so," said the friar.

"Oh, Friar!" Culca threw her arms around his neck.

"What, child?" the friar asked. "What is it?"

"Look." Culca pointed to the arrow that had pierced his robes. The friar's mouth fell open.

"Oh, mercy of God," he whispered. "These old robes stopped it." He looked back at the village, far away on the shore. "How could their arrows fly so far?"

"They flew on wings of hunger," the man closest to him replied. He picked up the arrow and pointed at the reddened tip. "Poison," he said.

"Why did they try to kill us?" Culca asked.

"They're cannibals," the man said.

"What's that?" Culca asked.

"They eat people."

Culca stared back at the village with wide eyes. People who ate other people? She'd never heard of such a thing.

They sailed in a wide circle around the cannibal village, and then paddled close to the shore again. Hours passed and all Culca saw was the beach and jungle. Finally, they passed a rocky point jutting into the water and Culca saw something she'd never seen before—a harbor filled with ships. There were great three-masted Spanish galleons with huge white sails, smaller sailboats with only one mast, and longboats rowed by slaves.

"Are these all the ships in the world?" Culca asked.

"Hardly," the friar laughed. "This is one tiny port. There are many larger ports. And many, many more ships."

On the hill behind the harbor was a city much larger than Culca's village.

"And I suppose this is a tiny city, Friar," she said, pointing at the low white buildings with roofs of red tile.

"Certainly, compared to the cities of Europe," replied the friar.

Culca thought for a moment. "How large is the world?"

"No one knows," the friar said. "There are parts that have not yet been seen. But we know it takes a ship three years to sail around it."

Culca was amazed. For most of her life she'd thought of the world as being not much larger than her little island. But from what the friar said, it was more enormous than she could imagine.

The outrigger sailed past the great ships in the harbor. Soon Culca could see people walking along the docks. Some were dark-skinned natives, others fair-skinned like the friar. Many were carrying sacks. One man led a large brown beast pulling a wagon.

"What's that?" she asked.

"An ox," the friar replied.

So that's an ox, Culca thought. She was amazed by each new sight. In just those few minutes she'd seen more people, ships, and buildings than she'd ever imagined existed.

Finally they reached the beach. While the villagers unloaded their goods, the friar took Culca ahead. They walked on streets paved with cobblestones and passed fountains spouting water. Soon they reached the marketplace. Hundreds of merchants sat under cotton tarpaulins selling brightly painted clay bowls and bottles, chickens and rabbits, wax and honey, many kinds of vegetables and fruits, cotton shirts and pants, earrings, buttons, and knife handles made of mother-of-pearl.

Culca saw spider monkeys and racoonlike coatis that were sold as pets. She saw hawks with bells on their legs. As she and the friar moved through the crowd, she clutched his hand tightly.

"What are these?" she asked, pointing to some noisy animals with pink skin and curly tails.

"Pigs," the friar said, "brought here from Spain, like horses, sheep, and oxen."

Everywhere they went the native peddlers beckoned them in dialects Culca had never heard.

"It's best to ignore them," the friar said. "If you answer, they'll only try to sell you something."

The friar stopped in front of a woman using colorful thread to sew a picture of a man leading a burro up a hill. Quickly and skillfully she sewed the picture and Culca watched as it came to life before her eyes. The friar picked up several needles and balls of colored thread the woman sold.

"Culca," he said, "I would like to give you a gift. Perhaps someday you'll sew as well as this woman."

But Culca shook her head. "She makes very pretty things, but this isn't what I like."

"Then what do you like?" the friar asked.

Culca led him to another peddler whose wares were spread out on a blanket on the ground.

The friar followed her and saw rows of metal knives in every size.

"Imported from Spain," the peddler said. "They won't shatter like obsidian blades."

Culca bent down and picked up a small knife. It had a wooden handle and a leather sheath.

"This isn't a suitable gift for a young girl," the friar said.

"It is for a diver," Culca replied.

The friar rubbed his chin. "If this is what you really want…"

He bought the knife and gave it to her. Culca stood on her toes and kissed him on the cheek. He quickly straightened up. Culca was surprised to see his face turn red.

The friar next found a peddler who sold seeds for his garden. While Culca waited for him, she noticed that the peddlers around them had suddenly grown quiet and were staring at something. Culca turned. Coming toward them were two young native men unlike any Culca had ever seen. The heads of fierce jaguars hung like hoods over their heads. Around their wrists and ankles clinked loose bands of jade and turquoise. Their earlobes had been stretched long and thin by heavy gold earrings, and each wore a gold ring in his nose. But what struck Culca was how the crowd parted for them and how they walked so straight and erect with an air of power.

"Young noblemen," the friar whispered in a low voice.

"But I thought the Spanish ruled," Culca said.

"They do," the friar replied.

Culca scowled.

"It must seem confusing," the friar said. "Now that the Spanish rule this land, your people must change. But change is best when it's gradual. Like everyone else, these young noblemen must do as the Spaniards wish."

Culca watched the young men pass through the market. "How else will my people change?"

"Come with me," the friar said, "and I will show you."

EIGHT

The friar led Culca to a long whitewashed building. Inside the air was cool and quiet. Two dozen native boys sat at desks and studied while a man dressed like the friar watched from the front of the room. Each boy wore a black and white gown and leather shoes. A few looked up and stared at Culca, but the teacher cleared his throat and they quickly looked down at their books again.

"This is a school," the friar whispered. "Just as you study with me, these boys are learning to read and speak Spanish. When they finish their studies they'll become teachers to other natives."

"Is there a school like this for girls?" Culca whispered back.

"Yes. They are taught to sew and cook and have good manners."

"Why aren't they taught what the boys are taught?" Culca asked a little too loudly, causing the instructor to frown at her.

The friar sighed and led Culca back to the hall. "Just like your people, my people have rigid ideas of what girls and boys are expected to do," he explained.

"Then the Spanish want to change us in some ways," Culca observed. "But not others."

The friar only smiled.

From the school they walked to the church in the center of the city. Culca looked up at it in awe. It was taller than the tallest palm tree. The point of its spire seemed to scrape the clouds themselves, and she had never seen anything as beautiful as the large round stained-glass window in front. Sitting on the ground near the entrance was something that resembled a great bronze cup. It was as tall as the friar and etched with beautiful designs.

"Why does this cup sit here?" she asked.

"It's a bell," the friar said.

Culca thought of the tiny bells the peddlers tied to the legs of hawks and falcons. Surely this couldn't be the same thing.

The friar pointed up at the church's spire, where several smaller bells hung. "The bells remind people to come and pray. Because this was the first Spanish church built in the New World, the cardinal of Seville sent this great bell as a gift."

"Then why don't they ring it?" Culca asked.

"It's far too large for this church," the friar explained. "Like many of my countrymen in Spain, the cardinal doesn't understand what life is like here…but come, let's go inside."

They climbed the stone steps of the church and went through the tall wooden doors. Inside it was very quiet. The stone floor felt cold under Culca's bare feet. Many candles provided light and the air smelled of beeswax. Culca had never been in a room so large. Long wooden beams stretched high above and the ceiling was decorated with beautiful paintings. A long aisle ran down the center of the room, and on both sides were rows of benches where people prayed with their heads bowed.

Culca was awestruck by the majesty of the church. But the mood was broken by the rustle of cloth and the rap of footsteps on the stone floor. An important-looking man wearing black and white robes passed, followed by several sextons in black frocks. The friar quickly bowed and motioned Culca to do the same.

"That is the priest," the friar whispered. "God's representative on Earth, and the head of this church."

Culca watched the priest and his followers disappear down a hallway.

"Wait here," the friar whispered. "I'll deliver my report and return for you."

The friar left and Culca sat on a pew in the back of the church. It was so quiet she could hear every breath, every scrape of a sandal on the stone floor. Near her a woman wearing a black Spanish dress and shawl stood up and turned to leave. She was short with brown skin and long black hair. Culca looked at the woman's face and was startled. She was a native!

A little while later the friar returned.

"Friar," Culca said. "I saw a woman. One of my people. She was praying."

"Then she's become a Christian," the friar said.

"Does that mean she's Spanish now?" Culca asked.

"No, she is still a native," the friar said. He could see that Culca was confused by this. "Come, there's more I want to show you."

The friar took Culca down to the docks where many slaves were loading a Spanish galleon with wooden casks of cocoa beans, and bales of tobacco and indigo. The dock was lined with crates of squawking chickens, and a dozen sad-eyed sea turtles lay helpless on their backs.

"Food for the sailors during their trip back to Spain," the friar said.

Culca marveled at the amount of goods still waiting on the dock to be loaded. Although the ship was very big, it didn't seem large enough to carry everything.

"Is there another ship to take some of these goods?" she asked.

"There are many," the friar said. "All the ships in the harbor are part of a fleet that will sail back to Spain soon. Many of my countrymen will also be on board."

The friar sounded wistful.

"Do you miss your country?" Culca asked.

The friar nodded. "I'm an old man and I've been away from home a long time. I have dedicated my life to God's work, but I would like to see Spain once more before I die."

"Then you shall," Culca said.

The friar smiled weakly and placed his hand on her shoulder. Suddenly they heard a commotion. A column of Spanish soldiers wearing metal helmets and carrying long spears was marching toward them. The soldiers were shouting and pushing natives out of their way as they made for the docks. Behind them were carts drawn by oxen. Culca stretched up on her toes to watch.

"There are only wooden boxes on the carts," she said, disappointed.

"Treasure chests," the friar whispered, "filled with gold and silver."

Culca stretched up on her toes again. Each cart carried three chests, and there were many carts. They were followed by more soldiers and a man riding a tall white horse. He wore a gilded olive jacket and a black hat with a red feather. His cheeks were round and red, and his hair was the lightest Culca had ever seen.

"The governor," the friar said. "He wants to make sure that the treasure is properly loaded onto the ship."

Another Spaniard rode alongside the governor. He sat very tall in his saddle and had red hair.

"It's him!" Culca gasped. "The one who came to our island and struck you."

"Yes," said the friar. "The king's treasure-master from the House of Trade. It's his responsibility to see that the treasure leaves the New World safely."

The treasure-master shouted orders at the soldiers who in turn shouted at the slaves. All other work on the dock stopped while the heavy chests were loaded onto the ship.

"Why do they need so much treasure?" Culca asked.

"Because," the friar replied, "they have forgotten what is truly important."

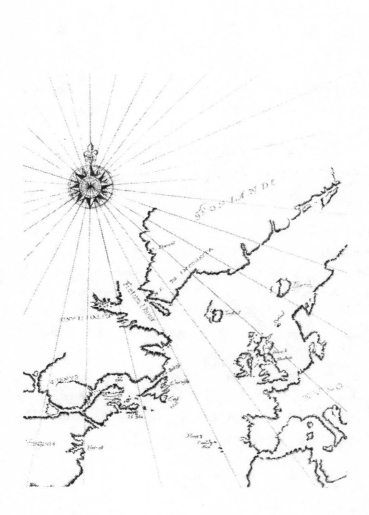

NINE

That night the friar and Culca rejoined the men from the village, who had spent the day trading in the market. Once again they slept on the beach beside the outrigger and in the morning they began their trip home. The outrigger was loaded with goods—obsidian blades gleaming in the morning sunlight, coils of new rope with the fresh smell of hemp. New clay pots for cooking corn were cushioned by straw in the bottom of the boat.

During the voyage home, Culca took out the knife the friar had given her. She knew that her mother would object to her having it so she tied it with two leather thongs to the inside of her leg under her smock, where Coatlicue wouldn't see it.

When they returned home the following day, a crowd of villagers was waiting for them on the beach. Culca quickly spotted Coatlicue. While the others unloaded the outrigger, Culca joined her mother and told her about the city.

"The friar took me to a school and a big church," Culca said excitedly. "And we watched slaves load chests of gold onto a ship bound for Spain!"

Coatlicue pressed her lips together and looked away.

"What's wrong, Mama?" Culca asked.

"You're young but youVe seen a great deal," Coatlicue said. "Soon our little village will be too small for you."

"But this is my home," Culca protested.

"We'll see," Coatlicue replied sadly.

Culca continued to climb the dirt path to the church every morning to study with the friar. One day he brought out a large map of the world and showed Culca the continent of Europe and the country of Spain, land of his people. He showed her Africa, the land where dark-colored people were found, and the far-off land of China, where a yellow-skinned race lived.

"Have you seen them?" Cuica asked.

"No, but others have," said the friar. "Explorers have circled the globe and a great deal has been learned. For instance, it was once believed that the Earth was flat. Now we know it's round."

"It doesn't feel round," Culca said.

"I know," the friar said with a smile. "But it is."

A loud bang on the church door interrupted them. The friar opened it and found Haab panting as if he'd just run up the hill.

"What is it?" the friar asked.

"Come! Look!" The boy pulled him by the sleeve. The friar and Culca rushed out of the church. In the great channel between the island and the mainland were dozens of Spanish ships, their white sails full and billowing in the wind.

"Faina sent me," Haab said. "Everyone wants to know where the ships are going."

"To Belize," the friar said. "And from there to Havana and then on to Spain."

Haab went back to tell the villagers. Culca and the friar stood and watched for a long time. Culca imagined the ships filled with goods and treasure, as well as crates of chickens and the sad-eyed turtles waiting helplessly for cooks to make them into soup.

The friar was very quiet. His face was long and the corners of his mouth turned down. Culca sensed that he wished he were aboard one of those ships sailing back to his home in Spain. She tugged at his robe.

"Let's go back inside," she said. But the friar shook his head.

"No more lessons today, little one," he said, and went into the church alone.

That night the wind blew hard and the palm trees shook and clattered. Culca lay in her hammock and listened to the approaching thunder. Soon she heard voices outside.

"Tulone!" Batab shouted. "A storm is coming. Help us pull the outriggers up and tie them to the trees."

Tulone went outside. Culca huddled with Coatlicue in the hut as the thunder grew louder and lightning cracked above. Outside the palm fronds rattled and coconuts thudded to the ground. Culca could hear small children crying for their mothers.

The wind blew harder still and suddenly Culca heard a loud scraping sound and she and her mother were showered with twigs and rain. A strong gust had blown the thatched roof partway off the hut.

"The church, Mama!" Culca cried, pulling Coatlicue's hand. Carrying pieces of thatch over their heads to protect against the rain and falling coconuts, they ran up the hill. Other villagers followed. Once again the friar held the church door open and offered them shelter.

The storm raged all night. Branches and coconuts battered the wooden roof of the church. Inside, the villagers huddled in the flickering candlelight and listened, unable to sleep.

By morning the storm had passed and the tired villagers left the church. Many palm trees were blown down and the beach was littered with coconuts, branches, and leaves. The roofs had been blown off many huts, and several walls had crumbled as well. Two of the village's outriggers had been washed away, leaving only the frayed ends of ropes around palm trees.

But the villagers were not angry. They were accustomed to the calamities of nature and the angry wrath of the gods. The devastation of the storm only meant that it was time to rebuild…again.

TEN

One morning soon after the storm, Culca was helping her mother when they heard wild shouts and saw Tulone race across the beach. Two Spanish soldiers on horses were right behind him! One of the soldiers snapped a whip, catching Tulone around the ankles and tripping him. The soldiers quickly jumped down onto the sand and began beating and kicking him.

"Stop!" Coatlicue shouted, running toward them. Culca grabbed a fishing spear and followed, but before she could reach Tulone, other soldiers on horseback appeared, brandishing crossbows and swords. One rode right at Culca.

"Run, Culca!" Tulone yelled. Culca jabbed the spear at the soldier's horse, but the soldier slapped the spear away and knocked her onto the sand.

"Let him go!" Coatlicue shrieked as she threw pieces of coral at the soldiers holding Tulone.

The men on horseback rode toward her. One of them struck her on the shoulder and knocked her down.

"Mama!" Culca ran to her. Coatlicue rose unsteadily, clutching her shoulder.

"Where are you taking my son?" she wailed at the soldiers.

The soldiers ignored her. Culca and her mother watched helplessly as Tulone was pulled to his feet and his hands were tied behind his back. Other soldiers came out of the jungle leading two more of the village divers.

"They must have come from the other end of the island," Culca said angrily. "To surprise us."

She had another surprise as the Spanish treasure-master came down the hill, pushing the friar ahead of him. The friar's face was bloody and twice he staggered and fell to his knees, only to be kicked and yanked up again.

"Are there more divers?" the treasure-master shouted at him.

The friar shook his head and the treasure-master struck him with a sharp blow to the back. The friar tumbled to the sand and the treasure-master held his sword close to the friar's neck.

"This time you'll tell the truth, Friar," the treasure-master snarled. One of the soldiers stepped close to him.

"Please, sir," the soldier said in Spanish. "He's a religious man."

"He's a liar," the treasure-master snapped. He pressed the sword against the friar's neck. "The truth, Father...are there any more divers?"

The friar trembled with fear and grimaced in pain.

"Speak, Father," the treasure-master demanded.

"That's all there are," the friar whimpered. "I swear on the Bible."

The treasure-master let the friar go. He mounted his horse and pointed at Tulone and the other divers.

"Take them back to the ship," he told the soldiers.

Seeing them lead her brother away, Culca could no longer restrain herself. "Stop!" she shouted in Spanish.

The treasure-master turned and frowned. "Who said that?"

"The king of Spain says we are free people," Culca yelled angrily.

The treasure-master gazed at her and smiled. "Who taught you to speak Spanish, Indian girl?"

Culca didn't answer. The treasure-master glanced at the friar, who kneeled on his hands and knees in the sand. Blood dripped from his nose.

"So this worthless bag of bones has done some good after all," the treasure-master said. He looked at Culca. "Yes, the king has said your people are free...and they are...until he needs them for gold."

The treasure-master turned away and joined the soldiers leading Tulone and the other divers down the beach. Coatlicue fell to the sand and wailed with grief. As the village women tried to soothe her, the village men surrounded the friar. Culca saw one of the fishermen pull out a knife.

"Wait!" she shouted. "What are you doing?"

"He told them who the divers were," the fisherman said angrily.

Culca quickly ran to the friar, who was still on his hands and knees.

"Get away from him, Culca," warned another fisherman. "He gave them your brother."

"But the tall Spaniard would have killed him," Culca said.

"The Spanish are devils!" the fisherman shouted.

"Not all of them," Culca yelled back. "The friar gave us food and shelter during the storm."

But the villagers were not swayed. The fisherman with the knife came closer. "I'll cut his heart out."

"Then you'll have to cut out mine as well," Culca said, holding the friar's arm tightly.

The fisherman stopped and looked at the others. The villagers slowly turned away. The friar sat up on the sand.

"You should have let him kill me," he muttered, wiping the blood from his nose.

"Why?" Culca asked.

"Because they are right. The Spanish are devils. At least they're devils to your people."

"But you're not a devil," Culca said.

Coatlicue came toward them, her eyes streaming with tears. "Where are they taking Tulone?" she sobbed.

"The Spanish fleet sank in the storm," the friar said. "The wind drove them onto the reefs at the southern end of the island. Tulone and the other divers will be taken there."

"Then he is close by," Culca said hopefully. "Perhaps he'll return."

The friar looked away and Coatlicue only cried. No diver taken by the Spanish had ever been seen again.

ELEVEN

That night Culca and Faina sat with Coatlicue, who cried for a long time.

"First they took my husband," Coatlicue sobbed. "Now my son is gone."

"Can't we get Tulone back?" Culca asked Faina.

"It is up to the gods," Faina replied, shaking her head sadly.

Later Culca fell into a fitful sleep. She dreamed of Tulone being chased by the Spanish soldiers on their horses, and of the wooden chests filled with gold. When she woke early the next morning she found Coatlicue packing a hemp sack with food.

"What are you doing?" Culca asked.

"I'm going to the other side of the island," Coatlicue said. "To beg the Spaniards for Tulone."

Culca sat up. "But you don't speak their language."

"I'll make them understand," her mother insisted.

"Let me come with you," Culca said. "I'll speak to them. Even better, let's ask the friar if he'll speak to them."

Coatlicue didn't argue, so Culca left the hut and ran up the hill to the church. The sun had just started to rise and she surprised the sleeping blackbirds in the trees, making them flap their wings and cry with alarm. The wooden door of the church was wet with dew as she rapped it with her knuckles.

The friar opened the door. He had a dark bruise on his forehead and his nose was swollen and red. "What are you doing up so early, Culca?"

"Will you help us save Tulone?" Culca asked.

The friar scowled. "How?"

"We're going to the other side of the island to beg the Spaniards for him."

"They won't listen," the friar said, shaking his head.

"Please, Friar?" Culca said.

"You've seen how they treat your people," the friar replied. "If you annoy them, they'll swat you away like a fly...I'm sorry, Culca. I don't want to see you or your mother harmed."

"But what about Tulone?" Culca asked. "They'll harm him. Please come with us."

The friar sighed.

"Please, Friar?" Culca begged.

78

"It's a long journey to the other side of the island," he said. "Especially for an old man like me. But yesterday you saved my life...so I will go."

"Oh, thank you, Friar!" Culca grabbed his hand and kissed it.

A little while later Culca, her mother, and the friar set out along the beach. There were trails through the jungle that would have made the journey faster, but the jungle was also filled with jaguars and other dangerous animals.

The sun glared down and the sand was warm under their feet. The friar grew tired, but neither Culca nor her mother paused to rest. After several hours they spotted some Spanish ships in the distance.

"Salvage vessels," the friar said. "Sent by the king to recover the treasure."

"Would Tulone be on one of them?" Coatlicue asked.

"Most likely," the friar replied.

Culca and her mother quickened their pace. The friar, who was already quite tired, fell behind. Soon they began to see debris floating in the water and washed up on the beach— broken yardarms, pieces of masts and sails, casks of water, baskets, barrels. Then Culca saw something that made her bring her hand to her mouth.

"What is it?" Coatlicue asked.

Culca pointed toward the water where a man floated face down, his white shirt billowing out, his long brown hair swaying gently in the waves. He was clearly dead. The friar joined them. When he saw the man, he said a prayer.

Soon they passed more bodies floating in the water. At first the friar stopped to pray for each of the dead, but as they passed more and more bodies, it proved to be an overwhelming task.

"There were more than thirty ships," the friar said sadly. "Here is the result of my countrymen's greed. A few become rich, but hundreds drown and leave their families heartbroken."

"Look!" Culca spotted a longboat farther down the beach. A group of sailors were scavenging among the debris. Culca watched one sailor stop beside a drowned man and remove rings and gold chains from the body.

"Ask them about Tulone," Coatlicue urged the friar.

But the friar, recalling his recent beating by the treasure-master, was reluctant to go forward.

"They won't know his name," he replied.

"You can describe him," Coatlicue said.

The friar didn't move.

"Please?" Culca whispered.

"Oh, all right." The friar went ahead. Culca watched him approach one of the Spanish sailors. She couldn't hear what he said, but the friar pointed to her as he spoke. The sailor listened and then shook his head. The friar returned with a grim look on his face.

"What did he say?" Culca asked eagerly.

"One of the treasure galleons, the *Santo Cristo*, sank in very deep water," the friar said, pointing out to sea. "The divers can't reach it. Already two have drowned and not a single piece of gold has been recovered. The sailor said they won't let any divers go."

"Then he'll die," Coatlicue cried. She kneeled on the sand and sobbed.

Culca fell to her knees and hugged Coatlicue. She felt her mother's shoulders tremble with grief.

"I'll save him," Culca whispered.

"How?" Coatlicue asked bitterly through her tears. "You're just a child."

"I'll find a way," Culca promised.

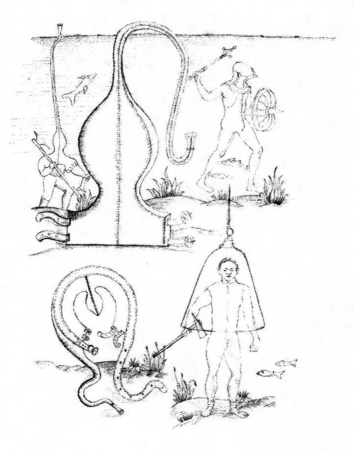

TWELVE

Night came and a full moon rose. Culca, her mother, and the friar trekked home along the thin white ribbon of beach. For the friar's sake, Culca and her mother walked slowly. Coatlicue was very sad and often broke into sobs. Culca held her hand and tried to think of a way to save Tulone.

By the time they reached the village, most of their neighbors were asleep. The friar turned toward the church, and Coatlicue and Culca went into their hut. Culca gazed sadly at Tulone's empty hammock and felt an ache in her heart. Then suddenly she had an idea.

"I must speak to the friar." She turned to leave.

"But we just left him," Coatlicue said.

"I know, Mama."

Culca ran out of the hut and found the friar trudging slowly up the hill.

"Friar!" she called in the dark.

"What is it?" He stopped, surprised to see her.

"I must look in a book," Culca said.

"Now?"

"Yes."

"Why?"

"Because."

"Can't it wait until morning?" the friar asked. "I'll very tired."

"Please, Friar, *please?*" Culca begged.

The friar sighed. "I must be very fond of you, little one. Perhaps too fond for my own good. Very well, come along."

Culca followed him into the church. The friar lit some candles. "Which book do you want to see?"

"The one with the pictures," Culca said.

The friar took the book down from the shelf. Culca quickly turned the pages until she found what she was searching for.

"Look, Friar," she said, pressing her finger down on the page.

The friar scowled. "I see drawings of men wearing masks."

"Underwater masks, Friar," Culca said. "If the divers wear these, they won't drown."

The friar felt a pang in his heart. He didn't want to disappoint her, but could see no other choice.

"Culca," he said softly. "This is only a drawing. Like men with wings and machines that fly, no one has ever seen anything like it in real life."

Culca stared at him. "But in Spain…"

The friar shook his head. "Not even in Spain."

"The Spanish build ships and cannons," Culca said angrily. "Surely they could make a mask."

"I'm sorry, little one," the friar said sadly. He touched her shoulder and yawned. "I'm so tired."

But Culca was not ready to give up. "The Spanish have taken all our divers," she said. "Without mother-of-pearl we have nothing to trade for the goods we need. The Spanish take everything they want, but they give nothing back."

"What you say is true," the friar said softly. "But there's nothing we can do tonight."

That night Culca's sleep was again filled with dreams. She dreamed of the drawings in the friar's book, and of the time she took him diving and he made the magic of air under the overturned dugout. She dreamed of their journey to the city, and her visit to the market and the big church with the great bell outside.

She woke and stared into the dark. Had the gods sent her a message? Was there a way to save Tulone after all?

The next morning she hurried back to the church and rapped on the door. When the friar opened it she rushed past him. The book of drawings was still open on the table and she stared down at the picture of the man standing under the large cone.

"Friar, it can be done!" she cried.

"I told you, Culca, these are only drawings," the friar said.

Culca pointed at the page. "Remember the great bell? A man could fit under it. He could breathe just as you did under the dugout."

"I don't know if that's possible," the friar said. "Besides, the bell is in the city on the mainland."

"Two of the village men are going tomorrow," Culca said, "to replace the goods that were lost in the storm. We can go with them."

The friar ran his bony fingers through his thin white hair. "Culca, please listen. This man Da Vinci is a genius. But many of his drawings are fantasies. Once the bell is submerged, surely the air will disappear or escape."

"No, Friar, it will stay," Culca argued. "Just as the air stayed under the dugout."

The friar recalled the last trip across the great channel and how queasy he'd felt.

"I'm sorry, Culca," he said. "I'm still very tired from the journey yesterday to the other side of the island. I can't go back to the mainland tomorrow."

"This could save Tulone's life," Culca insisted. "And help the Spanish recover their gold."

The friar shook his head. It hurt him to say no to Culca, but he couldn't go all the way to the mainland just to satisfy the whim of a young girl.

Culca didn't give up. All day long—while the friar tried to read or pray or tend his garden—she badgered him. And all day long the friar listened patiently, but did not change his mind.

The sun began to set and Culca knew it was time to return to the village for dinner. In the church the friar prepared his own meal of tortillas and beans.

"Then you'll let Tulone die," Culca said.

"I understand how you feel," the friar said gently. "But you don't realize the difficulties involved. To use the bell you would have to ask the priest for permission. And then the governor. They are busy men and don't have time to listen to a young native girl."

"But they'd listen to you," Culca insisted.

"Even that is doubtful," the friar replied.

Culca turned toward the door of the church. She was very disappointed with the friar. But it was not *his* brother who needed to be saved.

"All right," she said. "Then I'll go without you."

THIRTEEN

The next morning Culca told her mother she was going to the mainland. Coatlicue's eyes were still red and swollen from crying. She listened quietly while Culca explained how she thought she could save Tulone.

"But why should the priest and the governor listen to you?" Coatlicue asked.

"Because the Spanish think only of their treasure," Culca replied. "They'll do anything to recover it."

Coatlicue nodded sadly. "I no longer have the will to argue. Promise me you'll be careful and stay close to the men from our village."

"I promise, Mama," said Culca.

In preparing for the voyage, Culca made certain the knife the friar had given her was tied tightly to her leg. She also took the two pink pearls and the jade warrior Tulone had given her. Then she went down to the beach. The village men were ready to sail and they helped her climb into the outrigger.

"Culca!" someone shouted. She turned and was surprised to see the friar coming down the beach carrying something wrapped in an animal skin.

"This will help you," he said, unwrapping the skin and handing her the book of drawings. "Be sure to show them the drawing of the cone. They'll know the name of this man Da Vinci…God bless and keep you safe, child."

"Thank you, Friar." Culca placed the book in the bow of the outrigger.

The men started to push the outrigger into the waves. Culca glanced one last time at the friar. Then she turned and stared out at the deep blue water. The prospect of going alone to the mainland frightened her, but it was her only chance to save Tulone. The bow of the outrigger rose and splashed into the waves. "Wait!"

The men stopped. Culca turned around. The friar had picked up the bottom of his robe and was wading toward them.

"What are you doing?" Culca asked.

"Coming with you," the friar answered as he grabbed the side of the boat.

"Then you've answered my prayers," Culca said happily as she helped him climb aboard.

"Heaven help us both," the friar groaned as he sat down in the boat.

*   *   *

Once again Culca, the friar, and the villagers sailed toward the mainland. But this time the weather didn't cooperate. All morning the clouds grew thicker and the breeze stronger. By the time they reached the great channel, the sky was slate gray and a stiff wind blew in their faces. Whitecapped waves crashed against the bow of the outrigger. The friar looked pale as he huddled on the bottom of the boat.

As they paddled into the channel, the outrigger rocked and heaved. Soon Culca and the others were soaked with cold sea spray. The friar held on tightly and shut his eyes. Seawater dripped down his pale face.

One of the village men slipped a rope around the friar's waist and tied it to the outrigger.

"What are you doing?" the friar gasped.

"Tying you down so you won't be washed overboard," the man answered.

"Oh, Lord have mercy!" The friar started to pray.

Wave after wave crashed over the bow of the outrigger, flooding the boat's floor with seawater.

"Bail, Culca," one of the men yelled.

Culca started to bail with a hollow gourd. But each time a wave washed over the bow, more water came in.

"Friar, you must help!" she shouted over the howling wind. But the friar was busy holding on and praying. The waves kept coming. By now the outrigger was nearly awash. Culca watched helplessly as a pot of salt and several nacre shells were swept overboard.

"Friar, if you don't bail, we'll sink," Culca yelled. This time the friar opened his eyes, found a gourd, and began to bail with trembling hands.

As the storm raged, the village men fought to keep the bow of the outrigger headed into the waves while Culca and the friar bailed. Each time they finished bailing the water out, another wave would crash over the bow and flood it again. Their supplies and almost all their food were washed overboard. Culca's arms ached from bailing and she was wet and cold, but she couldn't rest or the outrigger would fill with water and sink.

As night fell, the winds began to calm and the waves grew smaller. The islanders were able to resume their journey, but the storm had blown them far off course. All night they paddled. In the gray light of dawn they reached the mainland shore and staggered up on the beach. They lay down on the soft sand and quickly fell asleep.

The sun was high in the sky when Culca woke to feel someone shaking her shoulder. She sat up and wiped the sand off her face and arms. The friar was kneeling beside her, looking very upset.

"They're gone," he cried, pointing at the spot where the outrigger had been. Only footprints and a long smooth groove in the sand remained.

"Back to the village," Culca said with a yawn.

"How could they leave us?" the friar asked. "I thought they were going to take us to the city."

"They lost their goods in the storm and had nothing left to trade at the market," Culca ex-plained.

"What will we do?" the friar asked.

Culca thought for a moment. "We'll walk the rest of the way."

The friar sat down on the sand and shook his head wearily. "You don't understand, Culca. I'm an old man. Two days ago I walked all the way to the other side of the island and back. All last night I fought the waves. I'm tired. I have no strength left. I can't go on."

Culca stood up. The men had left the book, a small bag of tortillas, and two blankets drying in the sun. She handed one to the friar.

"Then I'll go alone," she said. "You can wait here until I return."

The friar looked around at the empty beach and the palms at the edge of the jungle. He knew he couldn't survive there without her. He slowly rose to his feet, his body stiff and aching in many places.

"Lead the way," he groaned. "I'll do my best to keep up."

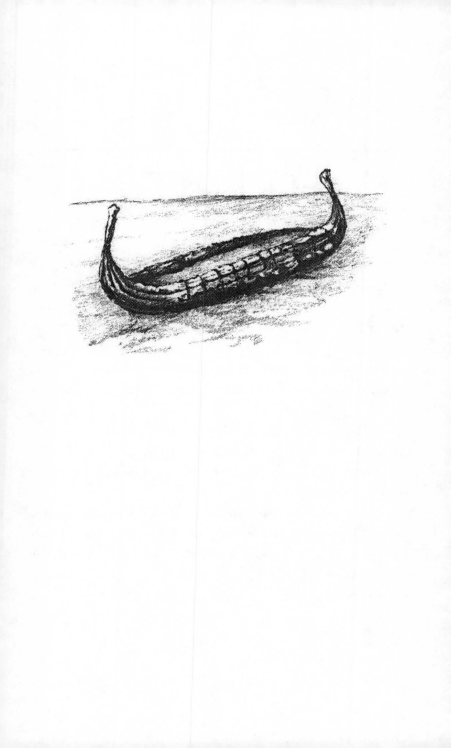

Fourteen

All that day they walked along the beach. The friar often lagged behind, but Culca was reluctant to stop. She didn't know how long Tulone would last on the Spanish salvage ship and she was afraid to waste any time.

Finally the friar fell to his knees on the sand. "Please, Culca, 1 must rest," he gasped. "At least stop long enough to eat."

"I don't mean to cause you pain, Friar," Culca said, kneeling beside him. "But I'm so worried for Tulone."

"I understand," the friar replied. "My heart wants to follow you, but my feet can't."

While the friar rested in the shade of a coconut palm, Culca climbed the trunk and cut down several big green coconuts. Then she hacked them open with the knife the friar had given her. She and the friar drank the cool coconut water and scooped out the sweet white jelly inside.

Ggrrooaarr! A deep, loud roar from the jungle startled them.

"Run!" The friar jumped to his feet and ran down the beach toward the water.

"Come, Culca!" He waved frantically at Culca who was still sitting under the palm, laughing.

"It was only a jaguar," she shouted back. "He won't attack us in the open."

"How can you be so sure?" the friar asked.

Culca thought for a moment. Perhaps the friar was right. And anyway, the jaguar had brought the friar to his feet again. Culca gathered her things and joined him.

They walked and walked. As the sun began to set, Culca looked far ahead down the beach and saw something that made her stop. She heard a grunt as the friar sat down on the sand behind her.

"I think we should stop for the night," Culca said.

"A very good idea," agreed the friar.

Soon night fell, and down the beach the cannibals started fires. Culca had not told the friar that the cannibal village was ahead because she didn't want to frighten him. The friar laid his blanket on the beach and shimmied about until he made a comfortable place in the sand.

"Every day you become more like a native," Culca teased him.

"And you, like a Spaniard," the friar replied with a yawn. He had eaten a good deal of coconut and Culca suspected he would sleep soundly.

"Aren't you going to sleep, too?" he asked Culca, who was still sitting up.

"In a while," Culca replied.

The friar closed his eyes and soon began to snore. Culca lay down on the sand with the book of drawings near her head. She imagined Tulone shackled and chained on the Spanish salvage ship. She thought of poor Coatlicue, sleeping alone in their hut, worried that she would never see her children again. She thought of her village and the hardships it would face with no one left to dive. Why? She wondered. What god gave the Spanish the right to come to her island and disrupt their lives?

Down the beach the fires grew dim. Culca yawned and closed her eyes. The thought of what lay ahead frightened her, but she had to save Tulone.

Culca woke with the first light of morning. The friar lay curled in his blanket, still asleep. She touched his shoulder. He woke slowly and rubbed his eyes. "Can't I rest a little longer?" he asked with a yawn.

"Only if you want to be eaten by cannibals," Culca said.

"What?" the friar sat up.

"Shh…" Culca put her finger to her lips. "They'll hear you."

"Hear me?" the friar gasped, looking around. "Where are they?"

Culca pointed down the beach. The friar squinted at the cannibal village. Culca watched as the memory of their last trip returned to him.

"How will we get past them?" the friar asked. "If we go on the beach they'll surely catch us. We have no boat and I can't swim. I'm sorry, Culca. But we must go back."

"We can't," Culca said. "We have no way to cross the great channel back to the island."

The friar paled. "Then all is lost. We'll be dinner for the cannibals."

"Not if we go through the jungle," Culca said, pointing at the green trees and vines beyond the beach.

"But the jungle is filled with wild animals," the friar said, his voice quivering with fear. "Only yesterday we heard the jaguar. If we go that way we may be eaten as well."

Culca took the friar's hand. "If we're lucky, the jaguar had a good meal last night and today he isn't so hungry."

The jungle was thick with vines, brush, and moss-covered logs. With no path to follow, their progress was slow. Brilliant blue and green butterflies danced in shafts of sunlight, and yellowbeaked toucans flapped from branch to branch.

"Do you know where you're going?" the friar asked as he followed Culca through the thick underbrush.

Culca didn't have an answer. She only *hoped* she knew where she was going. Still, she didn't want to frighten the friar. "I, uh, have the native sense of direction," she said.

The friar seemed satisfied with her answer. Deeper into the jungle they walked. The ground was soft and damp beneath their feet. The air was cool and moist and carried the sweet fragrance of jungle flowers. Sometimes the trees above them were so thick they blocked out the sunlight, making it seem almost as dark as night.

After a while they came to a large swamp. Jagged tree trunks jutted up out of the murky water like giant fangs. Clouds of mosquitoes buzzed in the air. Culca stopped.

"That way?" The friar pointed even deeper into the jungle. Culca shook her head. She was afraid of becoming lost. Then something on the edge of the swamp caught her eye.

"Look!" It was a small canoe made from bundles of reeds lashed together.

The friar frowned. "It's barely large enough for one person."

"It will get us across the swamp," Culca said.

"Across the swamp? Oh, no, Culca. We can't."

"Why not?" Culca asked. "We crossed the great channel in a storm. Crossing this swamp will be much easier."

The friar knew it wouldn't do any good to argue. He waited while Culca found two long branches to use as poles, and watched as she placed her blanket and book in the bottom of the reed canoe. Suddenly he felt a sting on his neck and slapped at a mosquito. Another stung his hand and yet another bit him on the ear. Culca was also slapping mosquitoes.

"This is worse than a storm," the friar complained. "Let's go back before we're bitten to death."

But Culca gestured for the friar to get in the canoe. The next thing he knew, they were poling across the swamp, followed by a swarm of hungry mosquitoes.

They poled for a long time. The water was still except for the ripples made by the canoe. The only sounds were the splashing of the poles in the water and the buzz of the mosquitoes. Finally Culca spotted a large tree on the far shore.

"We're getting close," she said.

"Thank God," the friar groaned.

They poled into the shallows under the tree. It had many thick branches and Culca eagerly grabbed one to pull to the dry ground ahead. But as soon as she grabbed the branch she knew something was wrong. It felt cool and too smooth. Then it moved!

"Look out!" the friar cried.

Too late! A huge python crashed down on Culca and the canoe, throwing both her and the friar into the shallow water. Culca felt her legs sink in the mud as the python wrapped itself around her, pinning her arms to her sides. The snake's body was as thick as a man's leg and Culca knew if she didn't escape it would slowly crush her.

"Get away, serpent!" the friar shouted, pulling at the coils, but the python was much too strong. Already Culca could feel the coils tighten as it began to squeeze the life out of her.

"The eyes, Friar!" she shouted.

The friar grabbed a branch and jabbed the python in the eye. The python hissed, but kept tightening around Culca. It squeezed her so tight that she could hardly breathe. The friar jabbed the snake again and again. Culca felt dizzy. She heard the snake hiss. Then she felt nothing.

Fifteen

When Culca opened her eyes, the python was gone and the friar was pulling her from the water.

Culca ached all over. "What happened to the snake?"

"He swam away," the friar said, pointing a trembling finger at the swamp.

"You saved me!" Culca reached up and hugged him. The friar blushed.

"With the good Lord's help," he stammered, helping Culca out of the swamp.

"The book!" Terrified that it had fallen in the water and was lost, Culca rushed back to the reed canoe. The book of drawings was still there, and she quickly unwrapped the animal skin. Inside it was dry.

"A true lover of literature," the friar teased.

Once again they began to walk. Soon they came upon a trail.

"This is a good sign," Culca said. "Hopefully it will lead us back to the beach."

The trail was long and seemed to wind endlessly. With the sun hidden by the thick trees above, it was difficult for Culca to tell the time of day or in what direction they were traveling.

"How much farther?" the friar asked.

"Just a little way," Culca replied, although in truth she had no idea how much farther they had to go.

Some time later, the friar stopped.

"What's wrong?" Culca asked.

"We've gone a great deal farther than a little way," he said. "If we don't find the beach before dark the jaguar may grow hungry again."

"Let's walk a little more," Culca said.

The friar sighed. "I've lived a long life, Culca. Should I perish in this jungle tonight, it wouldn't be a tragedy. But if you perish tonight…that would be a tragedy."

"We can't save my brother by turning back," Culca said, starting to walk again.

"You are a most stubborn young girl," the friar said, and followed her.

Soon the jungle began to grow less dense. Ahead, Culca could see sunlight through the thick vegetation and felt the air around her growing lighter and less damp. Her pace quickened with excitement and the friar had to hurry to keep up.

Between the tree trunks she caught glimpses of the sparkling blue sea.

"I knew we'd find our way!" Culca cried happily as she ran.

But then she stopped so abruptly that the friar almost stumbled into her.

"What?" he gasped. "What is it?"

"Shh…" Culca brought her finger to her lips and quickly crouched down. Through the thinning foliage she could see wooden huts. She felt the friar's trembling hand on her shoulder.

"The cannibal village," the friar whispered. "We must go back at once!"

"No," Culca replied.

"No?" the friar hissed. "Are you mad? We'll be eaten!"

"Maybe not." Slowly, quietly, clutching the book of drawings to her chest, Culca crept toward the village. The sun was high and hot and the village was very still. The morning fires of the cannibals were reduced to a few glowing coals and thin wisps of smoke rose into the sky. She could smell the lingering scent of scorched meat. Bones were scattered everywhere, some new, others sun bleached and old. She suspected the cannibals had just eaten a big feast and were now in their huts sleeping soundly through the afternoon heat.

"Come," Culca whispered to the friar. "I think we can sneak past them."

"You *have* gone mad," the friar whispered back. "I refuse!"

"Then I'll go myself," whispered Culca.

"*Most* stubborn girl," muttered the friar.

Culca stepped quietly onto the beach. The air was very still. The only sound was the lapping of the small waves against the shore. Being careful not to step on any bones or twigs, she and the friar slowly made their way through the village. But just as they passed the last hut, Culca froze. Lying in the shade was a scrawny yellow dog, its belly bloated as if it, too, had just finished a feast. Culca pointed to the dog and pressed a finger to her lips. The friar nodded.

They went a few steps more. Culca was almost certain they would get past the cannibals.

"Ouch!" the friar suddenly yelled. Culca spun around. The friar was hopping on one foot, holding the other in his hand. Then he sat with a thud in the sand.

"What is it?" Culca whispered, frightened that the noise would wake the cannibals.

"A thorn," the friar moaned.

Culca bent down and found a pineapple quill stuck in the bottom of his foot.

"Be still," she whispered, closing her fingers around the quill. With a sharp tug she pulled it out. The friar flinched in pain and a trickle of blood ran down his foot. Culca helped him up.

"Can you walk?" Culca whispered.

"Do I have a choice?" the friar asked as he started to hobble down the beach.

They had only gone a few feet when they heard a growl. Culca and the friar slowly turned. Behind them was the scrawny yellow dog. Its teeth were bared, and a low, fierce snarl rumbled in its throat.

"Move very slowly," Culca warned the friar. "If he barks we'll be dinner for the cannibals tonight."

Culca and the friar took a step back. The dog took a step forward. It growled a little louder.

"Do something, Friar," she whispered.

"Like what?" the friar asked.

The dog took another step forward. Saliva dripped from its sharp teeth. The friar picked up an old sun-bleached bone. The dog snarled again and came closer. The friar threw the bone, but his aim was poor and the bone flew many feet from the dog. Now Culca was certain that the dog would attack.

But it didn't. Instead, it raced after the bone. Culca and the friar looked at each other in amazement as the dog snatched the bone up in its mouth and returned to the friar's feet. Then it waited with its tongue hanging out and tail wagging.

"Throw the bone again," Culca whispered.

"Why?" the friar asked.

"Just do it."

The friar threw the bone. Once again, the dog raced after it and brought it back.

"He wants to play," Culca said.

"Wonderful," the friar said. "Now we can play with the dog until the cannibals wake up and eat us."

"Not if you throw the bone *that* way." Culca pointed down the beach away from the cannibal village.

So Culca and the friar continued down the beach, playing with the dog. In a short time they were far away. Soon the dog grew tired of playing and trotted back to his home, leaving them to continue unharmed.

It was almost dark by the time they reached the city. Culca and the friar were tired and very hungry. While the friar sat on a stone wall near the market and rubbed his sore foot, Culca went into the market and traded one of the pink pearls Tulone had given her for tortillas, beans, and sweet potatoes. She and the friar ate ravenously. Then, with full stomachs, they lay down and went to sleep.

When they woke the next morning, the friar got to his feet slowly and had a hard time standing.

"Your foot is swollen," Culca said. "You should see a medicine man."

"No, no," the friar replied. "Let's go to the church and get this over with."

The friar limped the whole way. When Culca saw the great bell outside the church, she squeezed his hand.

"Look! It's still there!"

They entered the church. The priest was giving a sermon in a loud voice from the pulpit, and the pews were crowded. Many candles flickered along the walls. Culca and the friar slid into a pew at the back.

"It's good to sit," the friar moaned, rubbing his foot.

When the mass ended the priest left the pulpit. Culca and the friar went down the aisle toward him, but a sexton dressed in a black smock stepped into their path. He was much younger than the friar and wore shiny leather shoes.

"Where are you going?" he demanded.

"We wish to see the priest," the friar said. "It's a matter of great importance."

The sexton frowned as if he doubted anything that concerned an old friar and a native girl could be important. He stared with contempt at their tattered dirty clothes and their bare feet.

"Go away," he said. "The priest has no time for beggars."

"We're not beggars," Culca said.

The sexton looked surprised. "You speak Spanish."

"Yes," Culca said. "And we must see the priest."

"No." The sexton shook his head. "The priest is busy."

He turned to go, but Culca said, "Do you know the fleet of ships that sank? One of the ships carried great treasure. But it's too deep for the divers to reach. I know a way to get the treasure."

The sexton turned and scowled at her.

"What she says is true," said the friar.

"Wait here," the sexton said. He went down the hall and disappeared through some doors.

He was gone for a long time. Culca fidgeted with the book and the friar rubbed his foot.

Finally they heard the sound of shoes rapping against the stone floor. The sexton returned, accompanied by the priest, who pursed his lips and looked at them impatiently.

"You know a way to recover the treasure of the *Santo Cristo?*" he asked, raising a doubtful eyebrow.

"Look," Culca said, opening the book and showing him the drawing of the man standing under the diving cone. "Using this, a man can breathe underwater."

The priest frowned. "We have nothing like this here."

"You have the great bell outside," Culca said.

But the priest shook his head. "This is nonsense. A man can't breathe underwater."

"He could breathe the air trapped under the bell," Culca insisted.

"There is no air under the water," the priest said firmly. "You're wasting my time."

"Wait!" Culca cried. But the priest turned and walked away.

"You must leave now," the sexton told them.

Outside, the sun was a round ball of warmth, but Culca was disappointed.

"He didn't understand," she said.

"His mind isn't open to the ideas of a young girl," the friar said as he limped beside her.

They found a place in the shade in a small plaza near the market.

"I must convince the priest that my idea will work," Culca said.

"Perhaps you should take him out in a dugout and tip it over," joked the friar. "Then he'll see."

That was impossible. The priest would never leave the church for her. But it made Culca wonder. What if she could bring something *into* the church? She gazed across the plaza to the market where a man was selling sparrows and other small birds.

"Friar!" she cried. "You've given me an idea!"

SIXTEEN

A little while later Culca and the friar returned to the church. Culca carried a tin cup and a small sparrow, with a thin strip of leather tied around its leg to prevent it from flying away. The friar lugged a heavy clay pot filled with water. Culca had bought both with the second pink pearl Tulone had given her.

Once again the sexton appeared. "You can't bring these things in here. Stop!"

"Gladly." The friar put the heavy pot down with a thud.

"We must see the priest again," Culca told the sexton. "I can prove that the bell will work."

"The priest is busy," the sexton snapped. "This is a very important day. The bishop is visiting. Take these things and go at once!"

His angry voice frightened Culca. Only the thought of Tulone kept her from running out of the church.

"Please," she begged. "My brother's life depends on this."

"That's not my concern," the sexton replied coldly.

"It should be," Culca said. "This is a church. If you don't care about people, who will?"

The sexton rolled his eyes and let his hands flop to his sides in frustration. Without another word he hurried away.

"He's going for help, to throw us out," the friar warned Culca. "We must leave!"

"No." Culca crossed her arms.

"Culca, please," the friar begged.

Culca shook her head. A moment later the sexton returned with the priest, who also looked very angry.

"Why are you here again?" he shouted. "You must leave at once! Go away!"

Instead of answering, Culca closed her hand over the sparrow and placed it in the water until only its head showed. It struggled and kicked furiously, but Culca held it tightly. Then she took the tin cup and placed it upside down over the bird's head. A moment later she submerged the bird and the cup under the water.

The priest and the sexton watched silently. Culca held the bird under for a long time. Finally the priest cleared his throat. "So you have killed the bird. Is that what you wanted to show me?"

Culca pulled the bird out of the water and removed the cup from its head. The bird blinked and shook the water off its wings. The sexton gasped.

"It's a trick," the priest said in disgust.

"No, it's not!" Culca insisted.

"Send them away," the priest ordered the sexton.

"Please, you must listen!" Culca begged. "It's not a trick. If you use the bell it will save the lives of divers and help you recover your treasure."

"Ridiculous," snapped the priest. He turned to leave, but Culca ran after him.

"My brother will die if you don't listen," she shouted. "My people will suffer. Is that what you want?"

"Of course not," a deep resonant voice said.

Culca stopped. Both she and the priest turned. Behind them stood a man wearing white robes embroidered with gold. On his head was a tall, almond-shaped headdress and in one hand he carried a long staff.

"The bishop," the friar whispered to Culca.

"Please forgive me, Your Eminence…" the priest stammered.

But the bishop ignored him. "Where did you learn to speak Spanish?" he asked Culca.

"The friar taught me," Culca replied.

The bishop glanced at the friar. "And why will your brother die and your people suffer?"

"It's nothing, Your Eminence," the priest broke in. "Just the wild musings of a heathen."

"She's no heathen," the friar said angrily.

"Let the girl speak," said the bishop.

Culca told the story of how the Spanish had taken Tulone. She told of how she'd heard that two divers had already died searching for the treasure of the *Santo Cristo*. Then she showed the bishop the drawing in the book, and told him how the friar had breathed under the overturned dugout.

"Is this true?" the bishop asked the friar.

"Yes, Your Eminence," said the friar.

Finally, Culca knelt before the clay pot and held the sparrow underwater again. When the bird emerged alive, the bishop frowned and rubbed his hand against his jaw.

"It's a trick," the priest said. "Some kind of Indian magic."

"Let me see," the bishop said, taking the tin cup from Culca. He pulled up the sleeve of his robe and plunged the cup upside down into the water. With his arm submerged to the elbow, he turned the cup over. A bubble of air quickly rose and broke on the surface.

"Remarkable." He stood up and shook the water off his arm.

"If the great bell were lowered into the water a diver could swim under it and breathe new air," Culca explained. "He could go deeper and stay down longer to search for the treasure."

The bishop turned to the priest.

"The king has ordered that the treasure of the *Santo Cristo* be recovered at any cost," he said. "I'm not certain this idea will work, but everything else has failed. I will take her to the governor and hear what he thinks."

Culca's eyes went wide. She grinned at the friar, who looked very surprised.

The governor lived in a large white house on the hill behind the city. The house was surrounded by flower gardens and rows of lemon and orange trees, their branches sagging with orange and yellow fruit. A servant led the bishop, Culca, and the friar through a tall iron gate and through a hallway into a large room with paintings on the walls.

The governor was sitting at a desk. Culca recognized him from the day she and the friar had watched the carts carry the treasure chests to the docks. On his pudgy fingers were many gold rings and a heavy gold chain was draped over his shoulder. Culca tried not to stare, but she'd never seen hair so fair or eyes so blue. Standing behind him a slave shooed flies away with a feather fan.

"To what do I owe the honor of your visit, Your Holiness?" the governor asked, eyeing Culca and the friar.

"I believe this young Indian girl may have a solution to the *Santo Cristo* problem," the bishop said.

Both of the governor's eyebrows rose and for a moment he gazed at Culca in disbelief. But knowing that the bishop was a serious man, he said, "Shall I call for Señor Velquez, the translator?"

"She can speak for herself," the bishop said, putting his hand on Culca's shoulder and gently guiding her forward.

In the presence of the governor, Culca's mouth felt dry and her heart fluttered nervously. Clearly he was a powerful and important man, the ruler of this land. Once again she told how all the divers of her village had been taken. But this time, before showing the governor how the sparrow could breathe underwater, she paused.

"Go on," the friar whispered. "Show him."

But Culca didn't speak.

"What is it?" the governor asked.

Culca cleared her throat. "Sir, I lost my father because he was a diver. Now you have taken my brother. Our village can't survive without its divers. I will only show you how to recover the gold if you promise to let my brother go and never to take divers from our village again."

The room fell silent. The friar looked aghast.

The governor's eyes narrowed. "You're either a very brave young girl," he said, "or a very foolish one. It's an insult for a mere girl to make such a demand. I've had men beheaded for less…"

But then he stopped and glanced at the bishop, who slowly shook his head. The governor turned back to Culca.

"All right," he said, "if you can show us how to recover the treasure of the *Santo Cristo,* I promise not to take any more divers from your village."

Culca began to smile, but the governor wasn't finished. "I'll make you a second promise," he said. "If you don't produce the treasure, you *and* your village will pay dearly. Do you understand?"

Culca nodded. She knew she was taking a great risk, but with no divers left in her village, her people would be destroyed anyway. And this was the only way to save Tulone.

SEVENTEEN

The next morning the governor ordered the great bell moved from the church. It took many men to lift it onto a cart and load it onto a longboat. Nearby, Culca and the friar sat in the shade and watched.

"For a moment yesterday I thought the governor would have your head," the friar said.

"But, Friar," replied Culca, "he wants the gold much more than my head."

The friar chuckled. "But what if you can't find the treasure even with the bell? What then?"

Culca shrugged. What had the governor meant when he said her village would pay dearly? Would he make them all slaves?

The captain of the longboat waved to Culca and the friar.

"It's time to go," he shouted. The friar rose slowly and could step only gingerly on his swollen foot.

"You should stay here and rest," Culca said.

"No, no." The friar shook his head. "I must go with you."

Culca and the friar sat in the stern of the longboat with the captain. Twenty slaves pulled on long wooden oars. Two more controlled the triangular sail. Propelled by wind and oars, the boat moved swiftly through the waves. The day passed quickly and as darkness fell, the captain ordered torches dipped in coconut oil and lit. The flames danced in the breeze and the captain told Culca and the friar that he planned to cross the great channel during the night and join the salvage ships by morning. Culca felt very tired. So much had happened and yet it seemed as if everything important still lay ahead. After dinner she put her head on the friar's lap and was soon asleep.

It was dawn when she woke. The air was cool and her clothes were damp from the morning mist. The only sounds were the steady *dip* and *splash* of the oars. The friar was still asleep, his grizzled chin resting against his shoulder. Culca rubbed her eyes and felt a surge of joy. In the distance she could see her island, and beyond it, the Spanish salvage ships.

They reached the largest salvage ship just before noon. Culca was in awe of its size. The hull was the height of five men and its sterncastle rose even higher. As the longboat pulled next to the ship, Spanish sailors and slaves looked down from the deck. Culca searched their faces for Tulone, but he wasn't there.

"Have you found any treasure?" the longboat's captain yelled up to the Spanish sailors.

"None," answered a sailor with a red bandanna on his head. "We're anchored over the *Santo Cristo*, but she's too deep. All we do is feed divers to the sharks."

The other sailors laughed. The one with the red bandanna pointed at a spot near the bow of the salvage ship where the pointed gray fins of several sharks cut through the water. Culca caught her breath. Was she too late to save Tulone?

"What have you brought us?" the sailor shouted down at them.

"A bell," the boat's captain shouted back.

"A dinner bell?" the sailor asked. "To let the sharks know when it's time to eat?" Again the sailors around him laughed.

"No!" Culca shouted angrily. "A bell to find treasure with. A diving bell."

The sailors stared down at her with surprised looks. They weren't used to native girls shouting at them in Spanish. Now another face appeared over the ship's side. With a start Culca recognized the Spanish treasure-master.

"What are you doing here, Indian girl?" he asked.

"I've come to help find the *Santo Cristo's* treasure," Culca replied.

The treasure-master frowned and looked at the longboat's captain. "Who sent you?" he asked.

"The governor," the captain replied. He pulled a white envelope from his shirt and gave it to a slave, who climbed a rope ladder up the side of the ship and handed it to the trea-sure-master.

The treasure-master tore open the envelope and read the letter inside. "What nonsense is this?"

Culca started to shout that it wasn't nonsense at all, but the friar stopped her.

"It's the order of the governor," the longboat's captain replied. "Would you disobey it?"

The treasure-master smirked. "Let them come aboard," he shouted. "And raise that stupid bell."

Culca climbed the rope ladder up the side of the ship with no trouble. Just before she reached the ship's rail, she stopped and looked down. Below her the friar was much slower. He winced each time he placed his foot on a rung. Suddenly his foot slipped. The next thing Culca knew, the friar was dan-gling from the ladder, his feet swinging feebly over the water.

On deck the Spanish sailors laughed. "Come on, old man," they shouted. "Don't let go or you'll be shark bait!"

Culca quickly climbed back down and grabbed the friar's wrist.

"Hold on!" she yelled.

The friar struggled to get his feet back on the ladder. But it swung wildly and his wrist was starting to slip out of Culca's hands.

"Hurry, Friar!" Culca cried. Just when she thought she would lose him, his good foot found a rung. He clung tightly to the ladder, gasping for breath.

"Thank you," he said, looking up at her. "I'll be more careful the rest of the way."

Culca climbed up to the ship's rail and pulled herself over. Suddenly the sailor with the red bandanna grabbed her by the arm.

"Throw her in the slaves' quarters?" he asked the treasure-master.

"I'm not a slave!" Culca shouted, trying to shake free.

"Let her go," the treasure-master said, looking down at Culca with contempt. "The governor has ordered me to assist you in recovering the *Santo Cristo's* treasure. What kind of magic spell did you cast upon him?"

"I have no magic," Culca answered. "I showed him how a diver could go deeper and stay down longer."

"Using a bell?" the treasure-master asked skeptically.

"A diving bell," Culca said. "But first there is one diver, my brother Tulone, who I must—"

"Silence!" the treasure-master shouted, his face turning red. "I've heard enough from you. You may not be a slave, but you're still an Indian. I don't care about your brother. You'll be silent unless I speak to you."

"But you can't," Culca protested. "The governor—"

The treasure-master pointed down at the shark fins circling near the bow of the ship. "Listen to me carefully, Indian girl. The governor isn't in charge here, I am. The sharks haven't eaten in several days. They must be hungry, but I have only two divers left and I can't spare them. I'm sure the governor would be very sad to learn that you accidentally fell off the deck and were eaten."

Culca stared at him angrily, but didn't reply.

Eighteen

That afternoon, Culca and the friar sat on the deck and waited while the sailors built a hoist to raise and lower the bell into the sea.

"The treasure-master said only two divers are left," she whispered to the friar. "Can Tulone be one of them?"

"Be patient," the friar whispered back. "If he's here, we'll see him soon."

The hoist was finished by midafternoon. A crowd of sailors watched curiously while the treasure-master ordered the remaining divers brought up from the slaves' quarters. Culca held her breath and felt her heart pound. Soon two divers were led to the deck, both wearing chains around their wrists and ankles. One was Tulone! Culca wanted to cry out with joy. When Tulone saw her his mouth fell open with astonishment.

"You are going to try this ridiculous contraption," the treasure-master told the other diver. He turned to Culca. "Go on, Indian girl, tell him what to do."

"When the bell is lowered into the water, stay under it and breathe the air inside," Culca told the diver. "When you're deep enough to see the *Santo Cristo,* swim out and look for the treasure. But when you feel yourself running out of air, don't try to swim to the surface. Instead, go back under the bell and take another breath."

The diver was quiet. Culca could see fear in his eyes. Like the others, he didn't believe that it was possible to breathe underwater.

The treasure-master held up a basket attached to a rope. "If he finds any treasure, tell him to put it in this basket and tug the rope."

Culca turned to the diver, who nodded to show that he understood what the basket was for. Then he climbed over the side of the ship and down the rope ladder. It took many sailors to lift the bell over the side of the salvage ship and lower it into the water. As the bell disappeared beneath the smooth surface of the sea, the gray dorsal fins circled it, but the sharks didn't attack.

The bell was lowered ten fathoms—the depth where the *Santo Cristo* was believed to lie. Everyone on the ship leaned over the side, watching and waiting. A barrel-chested sailor with a thick reddish beard held the rope attached to the basket.

Culca quietly left the ship's rail. Tulone was sitting on a water cask, his ankles and wrists in chains. He stared at her in amazement.

"How did you get here?" he whispered.

"It would take a day just to tell you," Culca whispered back. "How are you?"

Tulone shrugged. "It doesn't matter. Soon I'll be dead."

"Don't say that!" Culca whispered.

"The *Santo Cristo* is too deep," Tulone said. "The Spanish don't understand. 'Dive again!' they shout if we don't come up with the treasure. 'Again! Again!' Then the sharks come and the water turns red as they feed."

"What happened to the other divers from our village?" Culca asked.

Tulone shook his head sadly. Culca took her brother's hand and held it tightly. In the distance she could see their pretty green island. How she wished she and Tulone were home.

A long time passed and Culca began to worry about the diver who'd gone down to the *Santo Cristo*. Could she have been wrong about the bell?

Suddenly the bearded sailor let out a shout and began to pull on the rope. Everyone crowded around him. Hand over hand the sailor yanked on the wet rope, sending a spray into the air with each pull. Finally the basket broke the surface. Inside Culca saw silver candlesticks, copper plates, and a gold chain.

A cheer went up among the sailors. Even the treasure-master smiled.

"It's a miracle!" Tulone said.

"No," said the friar, rubbing Culca's head affectionately. "*She's* the miracle."

Culca hugged her brother happily. "Now you'll be saved. And our people won't have to live in fear anymore."

The bearded sailor emptied the basket and lowered it back into the water. Everyone waited to see what the diver would send up next. The minutes passed. A fork-tailed frigate bird glided high above and a large brown sea turtle swam near the salvage ship, then disappeared with a splash. As the sun moved slowly across the afternoon sky, the elation of the crew gradually turned to puzzlement.

"Why doesn't he send up more treasure?" the treasure-master wondered aloud. Finally he turned to the bearded sailor. "Bring up the basket."

Once again everyone pressed against the railing. As the basket broke the surface, Culca heard a loud gasp.

"It's filled with silver cups and plates!" one of the sailors said.

"I'm sure he didn't tug on the rope," the bearded sailor said.

"Perhaps in his excitement he forgot," suggested the friar.

"Send the basket back down," the treasure-master ordered.

Once again the crew waited. Culca sat with Tulone, clutching the jade good luck charm he had given her.

The sun turned red and fell slowly toward the horizon, but the diver didn't tug on the rope. Finally, the treasure-master ordered the bell raised. A dozen sailors and slaves grimaced and pulled on the heavy rope, slowly winching the bell up. When the bell broke the surface, the diver was gone.

The sailors looked disappointed, but Culca knew all they cared about was the treasure. She felt a pang in her heart as she thought of the diver. Surely he had drowned or been eaten. Had something gone wrong with her idea that cost him his life?

"The treasure-master would have made him dive anyway," the friar said to comfort her. "Perhaps he was destined to perish."

Culca gazed fearfully at Tulone. Her brother was the last diver left. Was he also doomed?

On deck, the treasure-master turned to Culca. "So, Indian girl, your bell seems to work. We have lost another diver, but we have finally reached the *Santo Cristo*. Somewhere in that ship are many chests of gold and silver." He pointed to

Tulone. "It's too late to dive again today. Tomorrow morning we'll use the last diver, and when we lose him, we'll use the slaves."

Culca clutched Tulone's hand tightly, but two sailors pulled her brother to his feet and led him back toward the slave quarters. Culca and the friar remained on the deck.

"I must figure out what went wrong," she told the friar. "If not, Tulone will die."

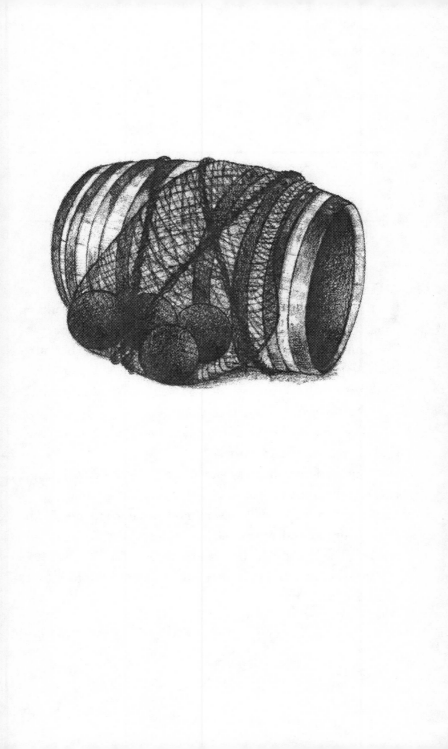

NINETEEN

Culca and the friar sat on the ship's deck. Above them the sunset slowly gave way to a black sky sparkling with brilliant twinkling stars. Culca wished she was like Faina and could read the stars for the answers to her questions.

"Perhaps the diver was eaten by a shark," the friar said.

"But the water didn't turn red."

"Then maybe he swam into the *Santo Cristo* and couldn't find his way out," said the friar.

"But he found his way out twice," Culca said. "Because twice he filled the basket."

"Then perhaps we'll never know what happened." The friar shrugged and massaged his injured foot. Culca's brow creased. The swelling had spread to his leg.

"Maybe the treasure-master will send you back to the city in a boat," she said.

"He would no sooner send me in a boat than call a native his friend," the friar replied. "He only wants the treasure."

Culca knew the friar was right. That was why they'd been left on the deck, cold and hungry. The treasure-master had no intention of providing them with food or a place to sleep. The night air was turning colder and Culca huddled next to the friar, hugging herself to keep warm.

"Tell me, Friar," she said. "Why is the treasure-master so cruel?"

"Like so many of my countrymen, he is blinded by greed," the friar said.

"If we find the treasure, will he become kinder?" Culca asked.

"I don't know."

The sound of footsteps on the deck interrupted them. In the moonlight Culca saw the bearded sailor coming toward them. She and the friar stopped talking. As the sailor came closer, she shivered with fear.

"Don't be afraid," the sailor whispered, handing them each a bowl.

"What is it?" Culca asked.

"Turtle soup and biscuits." He dropped two bundles at their feet. "And these are blankets."

"From the treasure-master?" the friar asked.

The bearded sailor shook his head.

"Then why did you give them to us?" asked Culca.

"Too many of your people have died," the sailor said. "If your diving bell can find the treasure and save divers' lives, then I wish you Godspeed."

The sailor stepped back into the dark.

"One never knows when an angel will appear," the friar whispered and started to eat.

The next morning the treasure-master and his sailors assembled on the deck. Culca caught the bearded sailor's eye, but he pretended not to notice her. Tulone was brought up from the slave quarters. His eyes were sunken and he looked tired. Culca knew he must have spent a sleepless night, dreading what lay ahead.

"Unchain him and lower the bell," the treasure-master ordered. As the sailors began to lift the bell over the side of the ship, Culca saw Tulone tremble with fear.

"Wait!" she shouted.

"What it is now?" the treasure-master snapped.

"Let me go instead," Culca said. "I know I can find your treasure."

"Fine," the treasure-master said. "I don't care who goes. If you don't return, your brother will go anyway."

Tulone began to protest, but Culca shook her head. She climbed down to the water and waited for the bell to be lowered. A few moments later the bell sank into the sea, trapping air inside. It was dark under the bell, and Culca could hear the sound of her own breath. As the sailors began to lower the bell deeper into the water, Culca swam with it. Her stomach tightened and her mouth grew dry with fear. She stared down into the dark green depths beneath her and reached to her thigh to make sure her knife was tied tightly.

The bell continued to sink, and the water around Culca became cooler. A curious shark swam by and Culca felt her heart race. But the shark wasn't interested and swam away.

The bell sank deeper and deeper and Culca had to swallow many times to keep her ears from hurting. The water was now dark and cold and she knew she was deeper than she'd ever been before.

A school of yellow snappers flashed below her. Another shark swam past. Suddenly something huge and dark appeared. Culca realized it was the *Santo Cristo*. Its masts were snapped like broken sticks and there was a great gash in its hull.

The bell stopped sinking. Culca tried to breathe steadily. The thought of swimming into the ship frightened her. But if she didn't, Tulone would die. She swam down toward the *Santo Cristo* and found an open window at the rear of the ship.

The room she entered was very dark. Because the ship was lying on its side, all the furniture inside lay in a heap against the wall. The legs of tables and chairs jutted out at odd angles. Culca felt around the jumble of furniture until she touched something smooth and round. A gold cup! Encouraged, she wanted to keep searching, but she was running out of air and had to return to the bell.

Culca made more trips into the ship and found two silver bowls, several candlesticks, and a heavy gold disk attached to a gold chain. She placed them all in the basket and tugged the rope. The basket began to rise and once again Culca swam back under the bell.

But this time, as she tried to catch her breath, Culca sensed that something was wrong. It was hard to breathe. At first she thought it was because she was tired from diving, but then she realized the air under the bell had changed. It had grown stale, and no matter how deeply she breathed, she still felt out of breath. Was this what had happened to the last diver? Had he tried to breathe air that was no longer breathable?

Culca's lungs hurt from the effort. She knew she must return to the surface. But how? She had no way of signaling the sailors to raise the diving bell, and it would take too long anyway. Her only chance was to swim.

She swam out from the bell and began to pull herself up the heavy rope. She was so deep she couldn't see the surface above her. Higher and higher she rose through the water, her lungs burning for a fresh breath of air.

The water began to grow lighter and warmer. Culca's heart pounded. Her fingertips tingled and her ribs throbbed. Up, up, up through the water she rose and yet the surface still seemed distant. She was tiring quickly. Each time she grabbed the rope it felt like her last.

The pain in her chest grew so great she thought her heart would burst, and yet from the warmth and brightness of the water she knew she was almost there. She had to let air out of her lungs for some relief, but now the desire to breathe was even stronger. She felt her lips part and tasted saltwater in her mouth.

At the very last moment she broke through the surface and gasped for air. She could hear the sailors above shouting at her, but she was too tired to try to understand. She took another breath. Fresh air had never tasted so good.

Above her the sailors continued to shout. Suddenly the words made sense—"Shark! Look out! Shark!" Two gray fins were circling close by. A rope splashed into the water near her. Culca grabbed it, but she was too tired to pull herself up. The sharks were closing in. Culca was terrified, but all she could do was cling to the rope.

The rope jerked upward, catching Culca by surprise. She gripped it more tightly and felt herself rise halfway out of the water. As if sensing it was about to lose dinner, one of the sharks shot toward her with its sharp white teeth bared. Culca clung to the rope and closed her eyes. At the last moment, the rope jerked upward again, pulling her clear of the water. *Clack!* Just inches below her the shark's mouth snapped shut.

Culca clung tightly to the rope as the sailors pulled her up the side of the ship and onto the deck. Dripping water and shivering, she felt Tulone hug her and saw the friar smile broadly.

The Spanish sailors looked at her with awe. Even the treasure-master seemed surprised.

"Why did you swim up?" he asked.

"The air in the bell became bad," Culca answered as Tulone put a blanket over her trembling shoulders. "I could no longer breathe."

"Then the bell won't work after all," the treasure-master said with disgust.

"But it did," Culca said, pointing to the gold disk and chain she'd found.

"That isn't the treasure I want," the treasure-master said angrily. "I want the chests of gold and silver...and I can't raise and lower the bell all day long to fill it with fresh air. At that rate I'll be old before the treasure is recovered." He pointed at Tulone. "You'll go next."

"But the air in the bell is bad!" Culca cried. "He'll die."

"That's not my concern," the treasure-master said coldly.

"If I may interrupt, sir…" It was the bearded sailor, rolling a large wooden barrel toward them.

"What is it?" the treasure-master asked.

"If it's not possible to bring the diving bell up for fresh air," the bearded sailor said. "Perhaps it's possible to bring fresh air down to the diving bell."

"How?" Culca asked.

"Watch and I'll show you," the sailor said.

TWENTY

"This is ridiculous!" grumbled the treasure-master. "A barrel filled with air won't sink."

"It will if it's weighted," replied the bearded sailor as he lashed heavy cannonballs to the barrel. Then he sealed the barrel with a cork so no air could escape while it was underwater.

"Pull the barrel under the bell and let the fresh air out," he told Culca. "Then tug the rope. We'll pull the barrel back up and send it down with more fresh air."

Culca stepped around the barrel. Standing on its end, it was almost as tall as she. It looked very heavy.

"Can you pull it under the bell by yourself?" the friar asked in the native language.

"I'll go with you," Tulone said.

"Can my brother dive with me?" Culca asked the treasure-master. "We'll find more treasure that way."

"You must find the treasure chests," the treasure-master said. He spread a large scroll of white parchment out on the deck. It was a diagram of the inside of a ship.

"I'm certain the gold disk you found came from the captain's cabin," the treasure-master said, pointing at the diagram. "There's a hatch with an iron ring in the floor. Pull the hatch up and you'll find the treasure chests."

"And if we find the chests will you let us go and take no more divers from our village?" Culca asked.

"That's what the governor said," the treasure-master answered. Then he ordered the sailors to lower the barrel of air over the side. Culca watched it disappear into the sea. Meanwhile, the friar sat against a mast, grimacing from the pain of his swollen leg. Culca turned once again to the treasure-master.

"The friar has been very kind to my people," Culca said. "He's old and sick. If we find your treasure, will you send him back to the city where he can be healed?"

The treasure-master's forehead furrowed. "You have many demands, Indian girl. If I grant this one, how do I know you won't ask for more?"

"I promise that is my last request," Culca said.

"So be it," said the treasure-master. "Find me the treasure chests and I'll send the friar back to the city."

Culca and Tulone began to climb down the ladder to the water.

"Remember," Culca said. "The first thing we must do is empty the barrel of air into the bell."

"I hope the sailor is right," Tulone said.

They plunged into the sea and swam down to the diving bell. The barrel hung in the water beside it. Tulone and Culca pulled the barrel under the bell. Culca pulled the cork out and great bubbles of air rushed upward.

When all the air had left the barrel, Culca and Tulone swam under the bell. Culca cautiously took a new breath.

"It worked!" she cried. "The air is fresh!"

"This must be magic," Tulone said, looking up at the inside of the bell.

"Finding the treasure will be magic," Culca said. "Come, we can't waste the air. With two of us breathing it will last only half as long."

She and Tulone swam down through the cold dark water to the *Santo Cristo*. They found the captain's cabin and began to trace the floor with their hands. Culca felt something round and hard. Certain that it was the ring connected to the hatch, she planted her feet on the floor and pulled.

It wouldn't budge. Tulone joined her and together they pulled. Slowly, the hatch began to rise! Culca peeked into the room below. It was very dark, but she could see the outlines of many treasure chests piled on their sides. She wanted to swim in, but her brother motioned that they should first go back to the bell for fresh air.

Tulone swam out of the captain's cabin. As Culca turned to follow she felt something slide around her ankle. Little cups of suction pulled against her skin. Suddenly she couldn't move. An octopus must have found its way into the treasure room. Already a second tentacle was sliding around her leg.

Culca kicked desperately with her free leg. She reached for her knife but a third tentacle went around her wrist and began pulling her hand away! She fought with all her strength, but the grip of the octopus was too strong. Culca was running out of air. Her lungs began to burn. She was doomed.

The octopus was slowly pulling her through the hatch into the treasure room. Culca felt bubbles of air escape from her lips. Even in her fright she couldn't help thinking how ironic this was. She'd finally found the treasure, only to perish at the very last moment. But at least Tulone and her people would be free. And the friar would go to the city where his leg would heal.

Suddenly a hand pulled the knife from her leg! Tulone swam past her and plunged the blade into the octopus. A great cloud of black ink spread into the water and Culca felt the tentacles let go. Trailing ink and blood, the octopus shot out of the captain's cabin, into the sea. Culca felt Tulone's muscular arms go around her as he helped her swim back to the bell.

Under the bell, Culca clung to her brother and gasped for breath. They were covered with oily black octopus ink.

"Are you all right?" Tulone asked.

"Yes…" Culca put her arms around his neck and hugged him.

TWENTY ~ ONE

Once they had caught their breaths, Tulone and Culca swam back to the *Santo Cristo* and tied a rope to one of the chests. They guided it through the hatch and out of the captain's cabin. The chest began to rise to the surface as the sailors pulled the rope from above. Tulone and Culca followed.

On the ship's deck, they joined the crowd as the treasure-master opened the latches and pulled the lid up. Inside, hundreds of gold coins glistened in the sunlight.

"Excellent!" shouted the treasure-master. Once again Culca hugged Tulone. At last they were free! They would go back to their village and never be bothered by the Spanish again.

The treasure-master turned to Culca and Tulone. Culca thought he would thank her, but instead he said, "Go! Bring me another chest."

Culca was stunned. "You said when we found the treasure we could go."

"When it is here on this deck," the treasure-master replied.

"But there are too many chests," Culca said. "It will take weeks to bring them all up. The friar is very ill. He won't last."

"Then I suggest you hurry," snapped the treasure-master.

"No!" shouted Culca. "You gave me your word."

The treasure-master squinted with anger. "Raise your voice to me again, Indian girl, and you *and* the friar will be lunch for the sharks. Now dive...or die."

Culca stared numbly at him. The treasure-master had lied. Tulone touched her arm.

"Come, little sister," he said softly. "It's better to dive than be food for the sharks."

That afternoon they brought up three chests of gold, but dozens more remained in the treasure room. Culca carried the bitter taste of broken promises in her mouth.

As evening approached, she crouched beside the friar.

"The treasure-master lied," she said. "If only the governor knew. He would keep his word and let us go."

The friar nodded and grimaced with pain. His leg was terribly swollen. Small beads of perspiration clung to his brow.

"Does it hurt very much?" she asked.

"It's a dull throb," the friar replied, "but not as bad as the pain I feel for you."

"Don't worry," Culca said, patting his hand. "Well find all the chests. Then well be free to go."

The friar smiled and took her hand in his.

"Friar, you feel hot," Culca said, alarmed. "You must be very ill."

"The warmth will comfort me through this long cold night," the friar replied. "Just as you have comforted me through this long journey."

In the dark a sailor approached them. Culca assumed he was bringing them food and blankets, just as the bearded sailor had the night before. But instead he grabbed her arm and yanked her up.

"Into the slave quarters," he said. "The treasure-master wants to make sure you'll be here in the morning."

"He knows I can't leave." Culca struggled, but the sailor squeezed her arm tightly.

"Those are his orders," he said.

The sailor pushed her through a hatchway and into a dark room filled with shadows and the odors of human confinement. A single candle flickered from a rafter, and the ceiling was so low that Culca had to bend to avoid bumping her head. Behind her the sailor slammed the hatch closed. All around her slaves lay on wooden berths, jammed tightly together.

Culca felt their eyes on her as she crept forward, searching for her brother.

"Culca!" Tulone whispered. In the shadows she saw his face among the others.

Tulone slid over and made a space in his berth for her. Culca felt like a caged animal.

"Have you eaten?" Tulone asked. "I have some crusts of bread. It's stale, but at least it's food."

But the air smelled so foul that Culca had no appetite. "Why is the air so bad?" she asked.

"The treasure-master nailed the portholes shut so that we wouldn't try to crawl through them and escape," Tulone said.

"How do you move about?" Culca asked.

"We don't," another slave replied. "We lie here until we are called. Sometimes when the weather is bad, days pass before we see the sun and use our legs."

"How can the Spanish do this?" Culca asked. "How can they break their promises and treat us like animals?"

No one answered her. Culca felt tears of frustration come to her eyes. She had worked so hard and taken so many risks…for what? To be made a slave.

"Don't cry, little sister," Tulone whispered.

"I've been so stupid." Culca sniffed. "Why did I ever believe the treasure-master? He *never* intended to let us go.

Even if we find all the treasure here he'll probably keep us to find treasure somewhere else."

"Shh," Tulone patted her shoulder. "Sleep. You'll need strength for tomorrow."

Culca quieted and tried to sleep, but she felt very sad. For the first time since her long journey began, she had lost hope.

In the middle of the night a hand shook Culca's shoulder. She opened her eyes. In the dark she could see the silhouette of the bearded sailor.

"Shh." He pressed his finger to his lips. "Follow me and be quiet."

Culca got up. Tulone was also up.

"Where are you taking us?" Culca whispered, but the bearded sailor only shook his head.

Very quietly he led them down a dark narrow hall and up some steps. Then he pushed open a hatch and they climbed onto the deck. Culca smelled fresh sea air and looked up at the black star-specked sky. In the distance she could see the dark outline of her island. The bearded sailor pointed over the side. Culca looked down and saw a small boat bobbing next to the ship.

"Be very quiet as you climb down," the sailor whispered. "Your brother and I will lower the friar by rope."

"Why are you helping us?" Culca asked.

"The treasure-master gave you his word," the sailor said. "And the friar is very sick. He must have care."

"But the treasure-master will be angry," Tulone said.

"Now that he has the diving bell, he can find others to get his treasure," the sailor said.

"I'll go to the city and tell the governor that the treasure-master broke his word," Culca said.

"That would be a grave mistake," the bearded sailor warned. "I saw the letter from the governor you brought the day you came. It told the treasure-master to use the Indian girl and then do whatever he wished with her. There was nothing about keeping a promise."

Culca was shocked. The governor had never intended to keep his promise either! "They are devils!"

"Some of them," the sailor said. "Now go before they hear you."

Culca climbed down to the small boat. Then Tulone and the sailor lowered the friar, who clung feebly to the rope tied around his waist. Culca helped him lie down on the boat's floor. He still felt very warm.

"Friar, I fear you are too ill for this journey," Culca whispered.

"As long as I am with you, I'll be fine," the friar whispered back.

Tulone climbed down and untied the boat from the ship. They waved to the bearded sailor and whispered thanks and then began to drift quietly away in the dark. Culca reached for the oars, but Tulone stopped her.

"Wait until we are far away," he whispered. "So that they won't hear us."

When they had drifted far enough from the ship, Tulone pulled the oars into the oarlocks and began to row. Culca sat with the friar's head in her lap. His eyes were closed and his skin was dry and hot. She cooled his forehead with a rag dipped in seawater.

"Is he very sick?" Tulone asked.

Culca nodded. "If we hurry, perhaps Faina can help him."

But without a sail their progress was slow. The stars twinkled brightly and the only sounds were the squeaks of the oarlocks and the gentle dip of the oars in the water. Culca smoothed the friar's thin hair. Suddenly he opened his eyes and looked up at her.

"Where are we?" he whispered.

"Going home, Friar," she said softly. "Soon we'll make you well."

"Don't forget what I've taught you," the friar whispered. "Teach your people. Knowledge will make them free."

The friar's eyes closed and he fell asleep again. Culca was very tired and also slept. When she woke, the sun had risen. Tulone was still rowing.

"Look." He pointed at the white beach and the huts of her village. A few of the villagers had spotted them and were waiting at the water's edge. Culca's heart filled with joy.

Then she felt the friar's head in her lap. His skin was cool and gray. Tulone shook his head slowly, and Culca felt her joy disappear.

As the boat neared the shore, more of the villagers came out of their huts. Culca saw Coat-licue running down the beach waving and shouting. Finally the boat came through the surf and the villagers ran into the water to help guide it ashore. Tears of happiness streamed down Coatlicue's face as she hugged her children.

That day the people of the village celebrated Culca and Tulone's return. They listened in amazement as Culca told the story of her journey to the city, how she met the bishop and the governor, and persuaded them to let her use the diving bell to find the sunken treasure.

"Will the Spanish come and take our divers again?" Batab asked.

"I can't say what they'll do," Culca said. "But now that they have the diving bell, they shouldn't need divers."

"That doesn't mean they won't need us for something else," Faina warned. "Like a storm, there's no telling when or why they will return."

"But we have always lived with storms," Culca said. "And we will live with the Spanish, too."

Finally, as evening approached, the villagers carried the friar up the hill to the little church. They dug a grave next to his garden and laid him down. The sun was setting and the sky was filled with pink and lavender clouds. As was their custom, they placed clay pots of food and water in the grave so that the friar would have nourishment during his journey to the next world. Culca kneeled by the grave and dropped in her jade good luck charm so that he would have money to spend.

Tulone and the other men started to fill the grave with dirt. Culca stood beside her mother and Faina. The old fisherman Batab stood nearby with the young boy, Haab.

"The village has only two divers left," Faina said. "Tulone and Culca."

"Can I learn to dive?" Haab asked.

"I thought you didn't want to," Culca said.

"There are many fishermen, but not enough divers," Haab said. "Without divers our people cannot live."

"Good," said Faina. "With Haab and a few more, we will soon have enough divers again."

It was growing dark. The men finished filling the grave. Slowly the villagers turned to go.

Culca waited until everyone was gone. Then she went into the church and lit a candle. She found the friar's garden seeds and brought them back to the grave. There, in the candlelight, she pressed the seeds into the freshly turned earth.

"Good-bye, Friar," she whispered, patting the soil down just as she'd seen him do. "I'll miss you."

She turned to go, but then stopped.

"And don't worry," she said as a tear rolled down her cheek. "I won't let the weeds grow."

0-595-34491-7

Printed in the United States
148573LV00001B/26/A